The Lazy Days of Temptation

by

Sarah King

Also by Sarah King

The Finland Mysteries Series
Sleepy Island Lies

ISBN 978-952-93-4577-9
www.sarahkingauthor.com

Chapter One

Tytti Vertainen held the letter of complaint up to her nose, a three-page lambasting from a disgruntled reader of the *Tapiolinna Times,* a sleepy island weekly in the Finnish archipelago. She placed it underneath her papers at the bottom of her work tray; then she pulled it out and looked at it again. If she left it down there, would she come in every day and remember it lurking at the bottom? There were things down there that had been there for years. Ideas for stories yet to be realised, cuttings and photos that would never be filed. This particular letter could skulk away like a rusty old bicycle at the bottom of a lake, quietly polluting the water with the oil from its chain.

Tytti was a writer, a journalist supposedly. Accustomed to writing about others' ruin, she felt angry, and even a bit hurt, at this attack directed towards her. Maybe she would tear the letter up; or better still, burn it. The stench of alcohol wafted her way.

'The President isn't visiting today. Why are you using the good coffee cups?'

Steadying himself Teemu, her boss, rested the fronts of his thighs against the side of her desk. Broken capillaries riddled his bloodshot face. Tytti crooked her neck to avoid the fumes.

'Or any day soon I'd imagine.'

'What's that you're hiding from me?'

'I'm not about to tell you if I'm hiding it from you.' She stuffed the letter into the bottom of her work tray.

'Oh whatever.' He swayed slightly as he went to leave then corrected his posture and turned back again. 'But as your manager, I should know what you're working on.'

'Stop bothering me. Paying me a salary doesn't mean you control me. I'm not your puppet.'

'Actually you are, and I want you to do what I tell you to do!'

'I know when something needs to be done.'

'You do not! You procrastinate.'

'I do not! I ruminate. It's important to carry a thought through.'

'We have deadlines to meet.'

'And I like to see them pass by.'

'You'll never win employee of the month with that attitude.' Teemu staggered as he turned and wobbled back to his office.

'"Team work makes the dream work",' muttered Tytti, watching his departing back with loathing.

Noted for his love of whisky and cigars, he was usually annoying, but now reaching new heights. She had seen his wife around and noticed that she had lost a lot of weight. Teemu had grumbled one day about how she was inflicting a healthier lifestyle on him and how he was fed up with healthy food and being told to exercise.

While hiding the letter to avoid Teemu's prying eyes, Tytti had spotted some notes on a feature she had started researching. The article had come to nothing, as usual. She had completed the official form required to proceed, but it had been returned rejected.

'He really should stay away from open flames. He might combust.'

Tytti laughed.

'Another coffee?'

The suggestion came from across the room, from her good friend Kai, sitting at the opposite desk.

'Why not.' She smiled encouragingly. They had known each other all their lives but their paths had diverged when each had left the island to study and Kai had taken a job in Stockholm. Now Kai had been sat directly opposite her, brought in as Managing Accountant to find a way to make the newspaper profitable. It did not matter that he was neither a manager nor an accountant, since his mother, Anna Tapio, owned the newspaper.

Looking down at that day's page in her diary, Tytti wondered whether she should ask Kai a few questions. After all he was the son of Anna Tapio who, the next day, was holding a grand opening at a local castle now converted to a luxury hotel. She was scheduled to go along and interview people. Apart from having to talk to the guests, Tytti usually enjoyed these large events as a good buffet was often laid on.

Kai walked back into the room carrying a tray loaded with washed coffee cups and implements, and set it down on the coffee table next to the little red sofa. Their tiny office had once been a sweet shop and the little red sofa had been skilfully squashed into the old shop window. It was just long enough for Tytti to stretch out her legs, and was a good place to sit and think. She could also watch people go about their business in the market square, a slatted blind keeping them from knowing they were being observed. Not that Tytti considered it spying: it was just to pass the time. Often, she would be intently watching one of the market traders neatly stacking vegetables when the seller, sensing her eyeballing him, perhaps, would look round to exactly the point where she was sitting.

Strange old world, thought Tytti. But did strange include that faint whiff of liquorice she smelt late at night when she was working alone? Liquorice was one of the favourite confections of the Finns. Maybe even dead ones. She hoped there was nothing in that.

'Just ignore Teemu,' Tytti said. 'He doesn't have a classy bone in his body. From now on, let's use these cups every day.'

'I was thinking,' said Kai, looking up as he carefully laid out the coffee apparatus, 'I was thinking I might be able to help you tomorrow evening. Take a few photos or something.'

As he said this, he set out the delicate cups, saucers, silver spoons, sugar bowl, silver tongs, jug of cream, gold-rimmed side plates and Tytti's old biscuit tin.

'That would be a good idea. You'll know who's who.'

'I've become really quite interested in photography, you see. I know I'm here as the accountant, but, well, I hoped, if it was all right with you, I could maybe take a few pictures now and again?'

Watching his face closely, Tytti saw that his heart really lay in photography and that he probably had little interest in accountancy. That was fine by her. She had never got round to reading that camera manual anyway. And the managing? Well there was very little that needed managing. Tytti certainly did not need it.

The wages, pondered Tytti, he must remember to manage the wages.

The previous accountant had managed to forget the payroll on several occasions, thus putting quite a strain on her and Denis's finances for the month. Yes, Denis. She was not sure if Kai had met him yet, as he often came in excessively early to do the cleaning. He was so stealthy that Tytti often forgot he existed herself. As a journalist, Tytti was a late riser, preferring to come into the office after a leisurely breakfast at around 10 a.m. Of course, her work often took her into the evening and the night, newsworthy events coming and going as they did. And if a print deadline arrived and a story was not quite ready, well, they could just shift things round a bit and put it into next week's edition. It did not matter — or did it? One of the items on the list of complaints was a comment on how many stories seemed to appear a week or two after the event. The complainant obviously did not comprehend how long it took for people to get back to her. But then perhaps should she be more urgent in her requests for information. Maybe not. Features, op-eds, whatever, took time to put together. They must be left to percolate, like coffee in a machine. No decent coffee ever came from a jar of instant.

'Okay,' replied Tytti finally.

Kai's phone rang.

'Kai Ta…,' he began, before he was interrupted.

Watching slyly, Tytti assessed Kai's appearance.

He's always been handsome, she thought as she watched a slew of emotions cross his face. He was tall and blonde like many Finnish people, but unusually his hair was almost golden in colour rather than the more familiar white blonde.

His mother's hotel, Tapiolinna Castle, was one of the finer castles. It had been built when praying was in fashion, and had more chapels than bathrooms. It was large and imposing and still had a deep moat around it. Many of the moats of Finland's smaller castles had dried up, and they now resembled misplaced follies — positioned on rocks next to waning rivers, lost to the undergrowth and nesting pigeons. Many had been abandoned by the soldiers centuries ago, when their payment, the beer, had run out.

Concluding her scrutiny, Tytti craned her neck and looked out over to the market square. She could see people meandering about with woven shopping baskets. She could just see her friend Ritva Lempinen collecting a bright yellow coffee mug from a table outside her bookshop on the other side of the square. Kai rang off and hurriedly began to put his coat on.

'Problem?' suggested Tytti.

'Sorry. Do you mind if I leave early?' replied Kai, a frown on his face.

'Go, go, no problem. I'll let Teemu know, and see you at the hotel tomorrow.'

Warped by the summer heat, the old sweet shop door creaked as Kai disappeared through it.

Tytti went around the desks and sat down on the little red sofa. As she sipped her coffee, she slipped off her shoes, pulled up her knees and considered the day ahead. Two short news stories, mundane to say the least. A cat stuck up a tree had had to be knocked down with a water cannon when a crane could not reach it. The cat had survived and the owner had been presented with a rather large bill, which he was now disputing. And then she had a court report telling of how a taxi driver had been convicted for running over a hedgehog. He had been fined 400 euros. Neither story would require Tytti to leave her seat or apply any great effort.

'Where's he gone? It's only half past ten.' It was Teemu again.

'No idea. He just picked up his coat and went. Thinks he owns the place,' said Tytti, keeping a straight face.

'Absolutely! I will have a firm talk with him. But, then again… his mother does own the newspaper.' Teemu's shoulders shrank just a little. 'What if he went back to his mother and told her what I said? Family members can be excessively loyal to one another, even if one of them is clearly in the wrong.'

'Still, I'd be quick to show him who's boss before he ousts you and starts to run the place. I wonder if there's been anything unusual happening up at the castle recently? It would be in the public interest to know.'

'Oh just leave it alone Tytti. Anyway, my wife just phoned and we're going out to lunch. I may or may not come back, depending on how I feel.'

Depending on how much you've drunk, thought Tytti. The door creaked as Teemu exited.

Tytti sighed. Men. They always left her to it. At least she would have a cup of coffee and a biscuit, so she could at any rate enjoy the peace and quiet.

Turning to continue her surveillance of the market square, she was startled to find someone's face pushed up against the window, looking back at her. She backed off quickly, splashing coffee down her front. Then the door slowly opened. Pushed at that speed, it made no creaking sound, and Tytti looked up from a coffee stain to see a rather dowdy-looking young woman standing before her.

'Can I help you?' she offered.

The young woman stood very still and wore thick glasses that made it difficult for Tytti to see her eyes clearly. She handed Tytti a piece of paper.

'I was just wondering, hoping really, that there might be a job opening here. You see I've just moved to the island.'

The piece of paper was a CV. Tytti scanned it briefly. The girl did have some experience on one of the free papers. A not-very-prestigious newspaper.

'I'm afraid there's no opening at the moment.' Tytti wondered if she should give the CV back. It was unusual for a job applicant to simply walk in and hand one over like this. Normally, these things would be done online, thus avoiding such awkwardness.

'Please keep it,' said the young woman as Tytti's hand hovered between them. 'Maybe something will come up. Goodbye then.'

Tytti watched her departing back. Her quietude had been interrupted, but Tytti was unaware, at that moment, exactly to what extent.

Chapter Two

Standing on the beach, Tytti breathed the scent of wood smoke coming from a nearby fire pit. It was close to Midsummer, the summer solstice when the sun did not set, and it was still warm enough at this late hour to be outside. In the evening light, she looked up at the castle-cum-hotel standing before her. From this side, it was more like a French château than a medieval fortress. A castle built in two different eras. A little earlier, and unusually, Tytti had spotted a security guard with a dog patrolling the outskirts of the bay.

Sipping her glass of champagne, she turned her head and watched a curl of smoke unravel. Around the barbecue, a gaggle of people were already forming a queue. Should she have a grilled sausage now or save it for later? They might run out. That had happened to her once before at a Midsummer Eve's party and the memory had never left her. Bending down to ease the stem of her champagne glass into the sand, she straightened up and used her free hand to steady a plate while she took a satisfying bite of Karelian pie smeared with boiled egg and butter. Then, tuning back in, she continued to listen to Juha, whom she knew vaguely, describe his working life at *Helsingin Sanomat*, a national newspaper based in Helsinki. From what she could gather, his life seemed to be in freefall. Tytti privately thought that working in a place with a fridge full of free chocolate could not be all bad.

'It's the pressure,' said Juha, leaning into her. 'It gets to you after a while.'

Leaning back to keep him away from her food, Tytti stared mutely. Weak, she thought, no backbone. Hearing a cymbal, she looked up towards the lawn, where a crowd had begun to gather and a band was warming up to play. Couples were joining hands in readiness to dance on the shiny white floor with its cheery reflections of coloured lights. Thinking it time she mingled a little, she excused herself from Juha, swiftly collected a refill of champagne and walked up towards the lawn. Easing herself through the crowd, she nodded hello to the people she knew. She could see Kai standing with Anna next to one of the terrace doors, and was just about to go over to him when a tiny old woman arrived at his side. Tytti recognised her to be Suvi-Tuuli, Kai's grandmother and a well-known artist who was famously antisocial and rarely left the castle grounds. Kai's face formed a look of apprehension as the woman stood on tiptoe and whispered in his ear. Tytti watched, transfixed. Suvi-Tuuli seemed agitated. Over her head, Kai's eyes locked with Tytti's. He smiled slightly and beckoned her over.

'Hi, Tytti. Sorry, could you please excuse me.' And Kai disappeared.

A well-groomed Anna Tapio nodded hello without smiling. Her platinum-blonde hair smooth and tidy, her make-up immaculate, she was kitted-out in a tweed Chanel suit with frayed edges and gold buttons. She had completed her outfit with a pair of Jimmy Choo high heels, but beyond all this beauty, she emitted an air of nothingness. Tytti unconsciously pulled down the sleeve of her ill-fitting jacket.

She doesn't seem to have much interest in seeing me, thought Tytti, feeling simultaneously disappointed and disappointing. Tytti had known Anna since she was a child, through play-dates with Kai. They had been the only two children who lived close together on that side of the island. Anna was famous on the island, not only for the castle but also her occasional appearances in the press. The *Tapiolinna Times* had reported on Anna and her exploits many times over the years. But Tytti had always found her to be cold and distant. Growing up, the Tapio children had been much closer to their stepfather, Simo, and had relied on him for the emotional support that, some might say, should have been forthcoming from a mother. As Tytti had grown older, she had secretly wondered if Anna was not, in fact, a narcissist. A person with no compassion.

There was an awkward pause. Tytti could

feel the bright eyes of Suvi-Tuuli looking her up and down.

Now, Suvi-Tuuli, Anna's mother, was another matter. She had always been kind to Tytti and had let them, as children, paint pictures in her studio.

'Well, it's good to see you, Tytti. You should pop by some time to catch up.'

I wonder how Anna could be her daughter, thought Tytti.

'Yes, I'd love to.'

Suvi-Tuuli was silent for a moment and they both listened to the sound of the music drifting on the air. Then the old woman surprised Tytti by saying, 'I've been thinking about your father. It was such a shame.' Tytti blinked and stood up sharply. What was she talking about?

'"Shame"?' she asked.

Suvi-Tuuli was quiet for a moment.

'Did you know, I was close to your mother? I taught her at school. It was so sad to see her pass before her time. Well, at least now she's at peace. It was probably best she died in the end. Of course, you were too young to really remember. You had just started nursery school. I remember your mother saying you were having problems settling in. A tendency to violence towards boys. And how do you feel about your father now, dear?'

'Er, fine thanks.'

'I hope you know that I don't blame him for anything that happened.'

'Er, okay.'

'Well, it's good that you seem to have matured in some areas. But yes, your mother. She was a beautiful woman. I guess that's rare in most families …'

Suvi-Tuuli talked on, her gentle lilting voice seeming to belie the comments she was making. More like she was talking to herself than to Tytti.

But why is she telling me all this? Tytti wondered. Then the thought that maybe she was suffering from dementia came into her head. She remembered reading somewhere that dementia could often bring back long-forgotten memories. But could they be true? How could something stored up for so long survive unadulterated?

Suvi-Tuuli had stopped speaking. There was a slight mist in her eyes. Then a strange smile spread across her face and she leant in and hugged Tytti. Tytti momentarily stopped breathing and did not return the hug. She felt like a rotten log being crushed into fragments. Then Suvi-Tuuli began to speak again in that euphonious voice. Tytti stood up straighter and lowered her shoulders to unlock the hug. She looked directly into Suvi-Tuuli's watery blue eyes. Her own eyes had also become misty.

'It's strange that you're talking to me in this way.'

'She was a good woman in the beginning.'

'My father has never talked to me about anything.' Collecting her thoughts, she wondered why Suvi-Tuuli was not apologising for upsetting her. Then, out of nowhere came the thought: I don't know my mother. Tytti felt a sharp pain in her throat… I can't remember her… Her own eyes continued to cloud. And then as if she had said nothing, Suvi-Tuuli continued: 'Yes, come by the studio. It would be nice to catch up.'

During the exchange, Anna had disappeared and Kai had returned with a camera.

'Kai dear, can you move the helicopter soon? I'm sorry but the outline is ruining the scene for my painting.'

Feeling distraught, Tytti tried to distract herself. She really should get a grip. The mere mention of her mother, and she fell to pieces. What was wrong with her?

She wondered about Suvi-Tuuli's comment about beauty being rare. Maybe Suvi-Tuuli had been speaking the truth when she had commented on Tytti's lack of good looks. Tytti's wide-set blue eyes, surrounded by barely discernible blonde lashes, gave the effect of an other-worldly china doll. A thin girl with pale skin, in her teenage years she had shot straight up like a Finnish tree with no pause for consideration of curves and bumps. She had been overlooked by the short island boys, and the boys at that British university had just stared at her long limbs and whispered. She had never felt particularly attractive, but had always considered herself to be at least average.

Then she brushed it off and her confidence stopped wavering. Her strengths came from a life of achievements and hard knocks, which had very little to do with aesthetics.

Tytti interviewed a few people on their thoughts about the new hotel while Kai took some photos. Nothing very challenging. People were on their best behaviour and knew to say all the right things. Now she felt that the evening's work had been done and it was time to go home. Stopping off at the cloakroom, she collected her cardigan. Not being the best of knitters, she had spent months one winter working on it. It was a nice pastel-green colour, not garish at all, and she was quite proud of her achievement. Perhaps the sleeves were a little long and the pockets a little high, but still, she felt proud. As the cloakroom attendant passed it to her, she was surprised to notice a long white envelope, which had been stuffed into the pocket. She immediately took it out and ripped it open. There was a hand-written note inside.

'Do you want to solve a murder?' it read. 'Look into the fire.'

Chapter Three

Tytti slowly rode her faded gold-coloured bicycle back home, the mysterious letter in her pocket. Now this was a new one! She felt a chill of excitement.

'Yes, I do want to solve a murder,' she said out loud. But whose? There had been no murders in Tapiolinna that she knew of.

Look into the fire, she thought. Was it a metaphor? Possibly not. There had been a fire at the castle about thirty years ago. An old murder, then, maybe? The handwriting looked like it had been penned by someone who had been taught formally. Somebody older. That, or a foreigner from some part of the world where meticulous handwriting was still valued. So the murder victim might be that Tapio man. Tytti vaguely remembered a story about a man losing his life in the fire at the castle. But as it was late, she planned to begin her investigation in the morning. Constable Mansikka-aho would be a good first person to contact. Yes, Constable Mansikka-aho. Her mind began to wander. She remembered it as if it was yesterday.

The phone had rung.

'Are you alone?'

Tytti had thought this an odd question.

'Yes, we have time to talk now.'

As Constable Mansikka-aho had started to speak, Tytti had slowly started to realise that this was not an informal conversation.

'… yes, the accident took place on the long road to the island. About the point where tourists stop to look out over the archipelago. The highest point. I'm afraid he… he…'

Constable Mansikka-aho paused. 'He was killed.' Then he added quickly, 'I'll call your father and tell him to come over…'

Tytti remembered her ears starting to buzz. She remembered scratching her head in surprise and looking in the mirror opposite. There she stood in a grey sweatshirt, holding the phone to her cheek. But now Henri was dead. She looked just the same as before, but how could that be so when her boyfriend was dead? How could he have died? It was such a silly notion. But as the day progressed and she had sat with her father, the shock started to subside and she began to understand. And that was when pieces of her had started to shut down. The beginnings of grief, nature's defence mechanism from pain, had slowly begun.

On what would usually have been a contented pedal, she began to feel a familiar tightening in her throat. By the time she arrived home, she felt somehow both numb and raw from such an emotional memory. Hurts long past resurfaced, like shell shock might for a soldier. Over the years, sorrow had turned to resignation, and then to indifference. She had tried to move on, as everybody had told her she must; but whenever she met somebody, a man who silently asked to be closer, those first vital threads of affection struggled to entwine, defeated by her grief. She could not love again. She just became sad.

She still tried to avoid that road. A road with many bridges, including one with a new length of barrier separating it from the deep water.

But who had been the woman with him, seated next to him in the car at the time of the crash? Her name had come out after the accident, but Tytti had never managed to find out much about her. She had not been from the island, and Tytti did not understand why she had been in the car. Nobody else could think of any good reason. An affair—that was what they said. She could only guess, both the best and the worst. His death had left her holding her breath, gasping with questions she never got to ask.

Chapter Four

Next morning, wheeling her bicycle across the
cobbled square, Tytti veered to the left and right,
around the stalls, her wheels going over spent
pea shells and the stalks of eaten strawberries.
She nodded hello to the vendors she knew and
avoided eye contact with those still keen to sell.
She could never get used to their quiet
desperation. They would say hello and then
stand silently, waiting for orders. Tytti often
wondered what was going on inside their heads
as they stood there with unblinking stares.
Some even smiled directly into your eyes, which
was even more unsettling.

She propped the bicycle on its stand and
pushed open the door to Ritva Lempinen's
bookshop. She could just make out Ritva's violet
rubber sandals and horizontally striped black
and white tights at the top of a ladder. Ritva's
little Shih Tzu, Lili, trotted over to say hello.

'Sit, sit,' called out Ritva, who had spotted
Tytti's approach from her perch. 'How are you?
I'll put the coffee on. I'm just relocating the
crime section. *Another* book has been stolen.'
Ritva was re-shelving the crime books next to a
new security camera. Thievery in Tapiolinna
was rare and Tytti had recently run a story on

how, for the first time in ten years, a book had been stolen.

'I'm quite good. And how are you?'

'I'm not good. Terrible in fact.'

Tytti thought she might know the reason why.

'So how is the dating going?' Tytti thought it best to get Ritva's favourite topic of conversation out of the way in order to gain her full attention. In her desperation at having exhausted the pot of available men on the island, Ritva had registered with a dating website. She had recently opened the café part of her bookshop, and Tytti thought that owning a bookshop with its own little café would have been just perfect for meeting potential suitors. At least you would know that your date could read, and liked coffee. You might even be able to select a mate based on his choice of book. Avoid the self-help section, move towards DIY. Tytti smiled to herself at the thought. And avoid those tea drinkers. Meet a nice solid coffee drinker.

'I'm thinking about deleting myself,' sighed Ritva. 'On the website, people can check a box between one and ten to vote on what they think of you. When the bookshop is quiet, I keep going to my profile and voting ten for myself. I must have done it a thousand times. But I can never seem to get my rating up. I just can't compete with those beautiful Ukrainian women.'

Unlike the sharp-cheekboned Ukrainians,

Ritva had an open friendly face with apple cheeks and light-brown hair, not unlike the features of a hand-made rag doll.

'And I've been using this useless book's advice with all the contacts I've had.' Ritva gestured towards the counter, where a hot pink book with aggressive typography lay. Tytti could see that the author's credentials included a PhD.

Does one need a PhD to understand dating? she thought.

'So, I see you're using a two-pronged approach then?' Tytti chose to tease Ritva when she might have chosen a more delicate approach and sympathised with her.

'Well, why not?' her friend demanded, becoming defensive.

'Good, good,' muttered Tytti, receiving Ritva's glare and easing back on the attitude. Ritva began to clank down the metal ladder, her red skirt with white flowers swishing around her knees. Her eclectic fashion sense made Tytti's head spin.

'So how about you. Have you met anyone yet?'

'Nope,' summarised Tytti. Tired from yesterday's long evening, she had no desire to discuss affairs of the heart. 'Actually, I came over for another reason. Remember I told you that Kai Tapio was coming back to the island? Well, he's arrived. He's our new accountant. He seems quite normal. Like his years at university and then working in Stockholm haven't changed him.' Ritva knew what she alluded to. Kai had been working as a trader at an investment bank in Stockholm. He could easily have fallen foul to the endemic arrogance in that field.

'Yes, yes, I've seen him!' said Ritva. 'He's grown taller and has filled out a bit, but his blonde hair is still the colour of straw.' Kai and Ritva only knew each other in passing.

'Yes. He reminds me of a newborn baby, all pink and fresh, even though he's the same age as us.'

'I think he's *very* handsome,' said Ritva.

It seemed that Tytti had failed to move the conversation along. She paused and looked sideways at Ritva. Checking to see if Ritva had a particular look on her face. A dazed look with a slight smile, perhaps. A look normally reserved for young girls who had just watched *Sleeping Beauty*. Like Tytti, Ritva was twenty-five. But unlike Tytti, she had been married twice. First, a shotgun wedding at sixteen after a pregnancy scare. And the second to a biker who, after the divorce, had left her with nothing but a bad tattoo. And now Ritva was casting her net for number three. No amount of bad experience could daunt her into not becoming starry-eyed when it came to men. Time after time, Tytti had watched her best friend hope beyond reasonable hope that this man, *this* man, would meet her expectations, and then be proved the fool when the romance came to a messy end.

Tytti remembered that as children, when they had played with their dolls, Ritva had always dressed hers up in white and married her to Action Man. Then, half an hour later, a knitted angel from the Christmas-tree decorations box would become her baby doll. About this time, Tytti had been putting her doll into the doll's house lift. Pulling the lift up and down and watching its workings in fascination.

She sighed inwardly. Ritva was a born romantic who longed to be happily married. Tytti would tactfully point out the indications that this or that man was perhaps *not* so interested in becoming happily married; but beyond grabbing Ritva, shaking her by the shoulders and yelling into her face that she was bonkers to believe in this person (which she, of course, would never do), she had not once managed to convey her message. And now, with Kai back — a man who lived in a castle, not quite a prince but still living in a castle — working just across the square, must be to Ritva like wafting honey under the snout of a newly awoken bear. But then, who was she, Tytti, to decide whether or not Kai might be that special one? They were all grown-ups now. Maybe she should stop being so judgemental. She knew that her own experience affected her estimation of men. Of course, her estimation of Ritva was another matter.

'Let's have some ice-cream with that coffee,' said an appeased Ritva, and she went into the kitchen.

Left to her thoughts, Tytti's mind drifted to Kai's mother, Anna. She remembered one time when Anna had driven her home after she had fallen over and hurt her knee whilst playing football with Kai. She recalled being allowed to sit in the front of Anna's large black car, and how she had watched the woman extend a slender ankle to press her toe to the accelerator. She recollected how the car had smoothly slowed, Anna shifting down a gear, as they approached the wooden bridge across the castle moat. Then she had accelerated, and the car, a Bentley, Tytti had later found out, had responded gently, flicking gravel from the road. The sunlight flitted through a canopy of leaves, occasionally blinding them to the road ahead, but this had not slowed Anna down. The tree-lined avenue belonged to Anna. It had been built at vast expense by one of the Gustavs, a family with deep pockets who had sailed trees north two centuries ago.

Just how rich is Anna? wondered Tytti.

Ritva returned.

'I've been thinking about the fire at Tapiolinna all those years ago. I read in an old newspaper article that Anna inherited the castle after her brother-in-law, Ville Tapio, died in the fire.' Ritva paused in the process of pouring the coffee.

'Or was murdered. I suppose it depends on how you look at things.' Ritva was prone to be a bit dramatic. But rather than correct her this time, Tytti stayed quiet.

'What do you mean?' she probed.

'Well, it's a bit suspicious, isn't it? Ville dies tragically and then Anna inherits the lot. I mean…' Ritva leaned forward and lowered her voice. 'Could Anna Tapio have been an arsonist? Could she have wanted to kill Ville in order to inherit? I wonder if she was questioned at the time. I bet nobody dared to suggest it, what with her saintly reputation and such, but, well, you know, greed can do funny things to a person.'

'The paper said they'd been asleep in different parts of the castle.'

'Well, that's convenient.'

'That must be the reason Ville and not Anna was killed. Maybe it was just an accident. No foul play was ever discovered.'

'So, what's all this interest in the fire now?'

Tytti wondered whether to broach the subject of the letter. Ritva did like to talk, and the news would be all round the island before she had had a proper chance to investigate. Something, she guessed, that her mysterious correspondent would not appreciate. No – for now, she would keep the letter to herself.

Chapter Five

Her coffee consumed, Tytti decided to walk across to the police station to see if Constable Mansikka-aho was in. On a relatively crime-free island, the police station was often closed other than for people to have their identity cards and passports reissued.

It's not surprising that the crime rate is so low in Finland, thought Tytti. She remembered Britain. A Britain without identity cards. All those criminals running around, who never actually existed. Here in Finland, things were as they should be. A tight control was kept on the population, and having to prove one's identity played a major role in this.

The door to the police station was unlocked and held ajar with a piece of wood. Constable Mansikka-aho was sitting at a desk, wearing the everyday police uniform of navy-blue coveralls, one large rough hand resting on his muscular thigh, the other tapping away at the keyboard with one finger. He looked up as Tytti entered.

'Tytti Vertainen. And how are you today?' Constable Mansikka-aho was from the mainland. He had come to the island at about the time Tytti had started working at the newspaper.

'So so,' replied Tytti. 'And yourself?'

Constable Mansikka-aho thought for a moment. 'Not bad,' he replied.

'Do you have a minute to chat?' asked Tytti, thinking that he did not look particularly busy — although one could never really tell, with his 'uniform face.'

'What's going on?' There was a sudden spark of interest in that face. Tytti and the constable often exchanged titbits of information that passed across their respective desks.

'The fire. The one at Tapiolinna Castle about thirty years ago. Do you have any information about it?'

The policeman paused to think and then stood up, beckoning Tytti over to sit in his chair.

'Now, what I am going to show you is, of course, confidential.' Tapping away at his keyboard, Constable Mansikka-aho entered a password. 'Here are the documents on the fire. I'll go and make us a coffee and you can have a look.'

Tytti eagerly leant forward. There it was. The old incident report on the fire at the castle, originally typewritten, had been scanned onto the computer. Tytti began to read.

'At 01:32 on Saturday 25th June 1984, a call came in from Anna Tapio (aged 18) reporting a fire at Tapiolinna Castle. The fire brigade and an ambulance were dispatched immediately. On arrival, Anna Tapio and Terhi Tapio (6 months) were outside the castle. Anna Tapio was highly distressed and explained that she had been woken up by the sound of crashing timber. Anna Tapio and Terhi Tapio had been asleep in the West wing. The East wing was burning intensely. At this point Ville Tapio had not come forward or been found and was thought to be trapped within the East wing. There was little rescuers could do once they arrived on the scene. The fire brigade tried to get the blaze under control for several hours but it was already advanced when they arrived. The top three storeys of the castle were on fire. It took until approximately 05:00 for the fire to be extinguished.'

A note had been added to the bottom of the page: 'Tapiolinna Fire Brigade state no sign of arson; probably a candle.'

So that's what happened, thought Tytti. Scrolling down, she came to the perfunctory coroner's report.

'After lengthy investigation (26th June – 8th July) of the remains of the castle and the surrounding sea, no body has been found and the deceased is judged *dead in absentia*.'

So they never found the body. His body, or the burnt remains of it, would have been washed away by the sea. Tytti shuddered.

Constable Mansikka-aho returned with two cups of coffee and looked over Tytti's shoulder.

'Yes—he was in the older part of the castle, the wooden section built above the stone base. It's been repaired to look the same. It overhangs the sea so the toilets could, how would you say—"flush".'

'Who investigated the fire at the time?'

'Jari. Since he retired from the police force, he's been doing the odd job here and there as a security guard.'

Of course, thought Tytti. Jari would have been the security guard at the castle on the night of the party. Maybe it was time to pay him a visit. But before that, there was something else that was still bothering her.

Chapter Six

Risto Vertainen was Tytti's father and vicar at the island's Lutheran church. He had raised her since infancy after her mother died from breast cancer when she was four. The mother she could not remember.

Tytti had grown up at a vicarage in a small stone house set back from the church. A church that, on Sunday, contained two rows of islanders, each sitting a metre apart, on pistachio-coloured, painted benches. She had always thought that if only these had been more comfortable, like the seats of the Helsinki cinema, then more people might come. But she did not tell her father this and the people rarely came.

As her father was the vicar, she had, without real reason, been considered a highly moral girl by the other islanders — an opinion that had carried into her later position at the newspaper. On more than one occasion, while growing up, a frustrated parent had been heard to mutter to her child to try and be more like 'Little Vertainen.' And certainly from the outside she had seemed serene. Her strongest memory as a child was of her father's thick fingers determinedly lacing her hair into fluffy pigtails before tying crooked red ribbons to the ends. (Later, when she had backpacked through Peru, the little girls had reached up to touch it and called it *blanco*.) But then Johanna, Ritva's grandmother, had arrived as their housekeeper, bringing Ritva along with her, and had taken care of the hairdressing.

Vestiges of her composure and manners still applied when it came to her father, and she was always polite, though unsmiling, to the many people he ministered to: the hopeless, the irresponsible and the just plain unlucky. As a teenager, her curiosity had been piqued whenever there had been a knock at the door, or the telephone had rung, to hear who had done what or what the occasion might be. When the Synod had sent over a new computer, Tytti had helped her father to set it up, and had surreptitiously read many pages of his diaries as she scanned and indexed them onto the computer. Her eyes had widened in wonder as she read about the villagers' many secrets, and she had made mental notes to check facts and words she did not understand. And then there had been the old people waiting to die, who came to church every Sunday just in case that week was their time. Some of them were not even that old, but had still been waiting to die for years. Her father had explained that these people had lost their way. They were nervously expecting retribution, but God did not really work like that. That was what Tytti's father tried to explain, anyway. To Tytti, morality was as black and white as the Finnish winter. But her father had always stayed up late wrestling with his conscience over the right pastoral advice to give or thing to do.

Overwhelmed by the thought of the tiny world she lived in versus the world around her, she had decided to investigate, and chose English as her degree, planning to leave Finland and see the world after graduation. But when it had come down to it, to the things that mattered, to the things that *really* mattered, she had been smart enough to recognise that the grass elsewhere was no greener than the pine-needle-covered scrub of Finland, and that she needed to stay and keep an eye on her father. A watchful eye, as he was far too primed to see only the good in people.

Tytti sat at a gleaming table stacked with fresh new bibles in the kitchen of her father's church. She thought she would take the opportunity to share a few cinnamon buns from the bakery and a pot of coffee with her father.

'Dad, what do you really know about the Tapio family? I've known Kai for years, of course, but I was wondering about Anna and her mother, Suvi-Tuuli. I feel that I don't know them as well. Maybe it's a generational thing.'

Tytti's father pondered.

'From what I understand, the Tapios are a family that have had many troubles but who have always come through them in the most Christian of ways.'

Tytti felt herself sigh. Her father, as usual, was being exceptionally naive. There must be more to them than that. She continued: 'I've calculated that you must have been twenty-five when the fire almost consumed the castle.'

'Yes, yes, we heard the fire engines and got up to have a look. It was a bit dark but we could see an orange glow coming from the direction of the castle from the window upstairs. We decided to follow the fire engines to see if they needed any help. When we got there, things were out of control. There were firemen everywhere. Two fire engines spraying water. The fire was raging. Even from our far-off position, we could still feel the heat. And the police never found out how it started. What did your newspaper say? I suppose you know more about these things than I do. And then Anna stayed and restored the castle. What a task for a young woman! And what a woman!'

Tytti had always suspected that her father had rather a crush on Anna. He had been alone now for a long time, ever since her mother had died, and he and many of the other island men seemed to feel a similar way towards her.

'I found the pages on the fire.'

Tytti unfolded the printout and handed it to Risto.

'*Castle Destroyed by Fire, One Dead*,' read the headline. And then: 'In the early hours of

Sunday morning, a fire devastated Tapiolinna Castle. After four hours, the blaze was slowly brought under control. Ville Tapio, the castle owner, was thought to have been asleep in the East wing. The fire took hold of this section and he became a victim of the flames. All other residents of the castle escaped unhurt. The cause of the fire has not yet been determined.' There was no new information to be gleaned.

On the next page, the paper had gone on to publish a feature on the residents of the castle. It mentioned Suvi-Tuuli, who had painted a wedding portrait of Anna and Heike Tapio, Anna's late husband. The portrait had been printed.

'Do you remember, Johanna used to be housekeeper for the Tapio family before she came to us? This was way back when it was just the twin boys, Ville and Heike, and their father, Karl. A very strange bunch, she said. No sign of the mother, and a father, who tried to keep his two boys locked away from the world by home-schooling them. They were plenty good at escaping, though. Then Heike became lost while ice fishing. He was only sixteen when it happened. Then there was just Ville left to inherit everything when his father died a year later. Johanna used to swear that those boys never had any interest in girls until they met Anna.' The picture had been the last one of Heike Tapio. A handsome, dark-haired man who had died when Anna had still been pregnant with Terhi.

Not everything in this world is about love, thought Tytti in annoyance. She got fed up with the way things always seemed to come back to love. How in this case her direct journalistic questioning had turned out to be another quixotic conversation.

'How did Anna and the Tapio boys meet?'

'Probably at a crayfish party. When they turned sixteen, Johanna said, they became bold about their jaunts outside. They would have been sixteen or so when they first saw Anna. Anna was stunning as a young woman and apparently Heike fell for her the moment he met her.'

How romantic, thought Tytti, before correcting herself. She loathed being influenced by the sentimental nature of others.

Risto stopped, and looked away, a little embarrassed that he had followed Anna Tapio's romantic life so obviously. There was also something else on his mind, and he was not sure how to share it. But then, this might be the only opening he would get: sadly, Tytti was not one to visit without reason anymore.

'How well do you know Suvi-Tuuli Tapio?' asked Tytti. She knew Suvi-Tuuli to be something of a hermit, but she also knew that she went to church.

Half-hearing, half-ignoring his daughter, Risto took his chance and blurted: 'I worry about you. I fear that you have lost your trust in people.'

Tytti looked away. It was unusual for her father to approach the subject of emotions — when it came to her, anyway — so openly. He usually kept his thoughts on their small family to himself. But now criticism was forthcoming.

'I fear that since Henri died under suspicion, of, well, you know what, you have, quite naturally, lost faith in men; but I also think you have begun to lose faith in people in general. What's going on?'

Tytti froze, feeling the shock of a parent's criticism so much more than that of any other person.

'I... I don't know, Daddy.' She felt relieved to utter the words. She was close to her father, and trusted him above all others. 'I'm the same as usual — life is the same as usual.' Her decline had been so gradual that she had felt no sudden change. 'Anyway,' the outburst came harshly, 'people *are* untrustworthy. They are stupid and greedy! Look at all these horrific news stories! Murders, kidnappings...'

'Well, yes, these are sad, yet extreme, examples,' her father interrupted before Tytti could hit her stride. 'Nobody around here has committed murder.' After years of practice, Risto kept his cool.

'But they might have...' Tytti paused. Should she tell her father about the tip-off? 'And then there are the people I meet through work. The egocentric, overly-ambitious people who want press coverage to sell their products; the grief-stricken refusing to talk. All these people are difficult — and please don't tell me that they have their own problems, because I don't really care!'

'Tytti, you have become hardened. The world just isn't full of people that one-dimensional. Every one of those people just wants some food to eat, a place to stay… we are all the same in that respect.'

'Are we?' Tytti could feel her irritation rising. She was confused and anxious about what her father thought of her. Somewhere deep inside she knew him to be right, she just could not bear to let go of her stance. Or was it that she was so used to agreeing with him? Maybe it was time to become more independent. His comments had increased her hurt, as they came from a man she loved. And the hurt had turned to anger. Then the words 'physical wounds are finite, emotional wounds go on and on' flashed in her mind, she did not know from where.

'Well, please don't lose faith in faith itself. Then you really will have gone off course. As Christians, we are called to weep with those who weep. We must welcome emotional pain, as it results from empathy. If we grow numb to the suffering around us, we have lost our humanity,' said Risto the vicar. 'What's all this about anyway? Why are you so interested in the Tapio family?'

He had given up. Tytti wondered whether she should share the tip-off about the fire with her father. She trusted that he would keep it a secret, but he was prone to worry about her. Why she did not know, seeing as her job at the newspaper was so mundane.

'Oh, nothing important.' She had decided. Now was not the time to discuss Suvi-Tuuli's comments. The atmosphere was still raw. She wondered if her father blamed himself for her being so independent. She knew he felt guilty about spending so much time on church matters when she was growing up. There had been no mother as a role model, and he felt he should have taken up the slack more often, rather than just leaving her home alone with her developing moods — especially as Finnish children took themselves to and from school by the age of seven and then stayed home by themselves until their parents returned from wherever. And as school finished at 1 p.m. at the latest, this left a large chunk of the day for reflection. Tytti had avoided the after-school clubs and grown up something of a loner.

He's had a rough time really, she thought. She remembered the time her father told her that Henri had been stealing money from her. He had seen him take it from her purse. At first, the boyfriend had blackmailed Risto into not telling her, saying that it had been a mistake, that he would never do it again, that it would hurt her to know the truth. But after the car accident, her father told her. He had said that he had prayed about it since it happened. That he had prayed for a solution. But then Henri had died anyway. And then a part of her father could not help but wonder whether his prayer had been answered.

Chapter Seven

The next day, deciding on discretion, Tytti arrived by bicycle at the private entrance to the castle. Her bicycle was, after years of carefree journeying, a bit battered these days, but it still had a comfortable, if worn, seat, and the high handlebars allowed her to sit very upright, as if pedalling a weaving machine.

While catching her breath after the dusty ride, Tytti gazed at the sunlight flashing over the sea. Facing directly into the sun, she closed her eyes and could make out circles of translucent light reflecting from the ends of her eyelashes. As she opened them, she watched a squabble of seagulls hover low, curved and dark. As the squabble spotted a shoal of fish, it began to look menacing, the birds darting wildly, like fish-eating bats. A cloud crossed the sun and Tytti shivered.

Wheels crunching on the gravel driveway made her jump. A filthy police van had drawn up just in front of the castle's main door. Tytti stood quietly poised on her bicycle as the doors slammed shut and Constable Mansikka-aho and a woman got out. Tytti quickly dismounted and gently rested the handlebars against a rock. It was time to begin her observations. As the

woman pulled on the wrought iron bell, Tytti
decided that she was somewhat assertive, maybe
even controlling. Constable Mansikka-aho stood
back, in his usual relaxed position. Anna
opened the door almost immediately. Gazing
over the two official heads, she frowned as she
spotted Tytti. Kai poked his head round the
door.

'Tytti… er… how nice to see you. Do come
in.'

'Er, hello, well, I just stopped off… er,
stopped off…'

Anna glared at her angrily.

'Kai! How dare you not tell me that the
police and Tytti were coming over! You stupid
boy!' Kai looked affronted. Turning towards
Constable Mansikka-aho, she continued in a far
more honeyed tone. 'I don't want any kind of
trouble now that the hotel is up and running.'

Anna was fuming. She had just gleaned
from a suspiciously acting Kai that, bizarrely,
there was a skull wedged in the oak tree on the
lawn. He had phoned the police after first
phoning Tytti. This would be news.

Anna is livid, thought Tytti in surprise.
Why be so upset about, well, nothing, at the
moment? The skull was yet to be investigated.

'I didn't mention it to protect her,'
whispered Kai under his breath. 'I thought we
should have more information before I got her
involved.'

Or you wanted to avoid a confrontation with

you mother for as long as possible, thought
Tytti.

'And who are you?' Anna asked, staring at
the woman in the suit.

'This is Dr Wahlroos,' said Constable
Mansikka-aho, as formally as he could.

'They're just here to collect a silly bone,
Mother. The one Jari's dog sniffed out at the
opening party.'

'A skull, actually,' said Constable Mansikka-
aho.

'A cranium, actually. There is no jawbone,'
interrupted Dr Wahlroos.

'Well, if it looks like a human skull, I'd say
that it probably is a human skull,' Anna said
impatiently.

What would it be like to be so rich and
thoughtless that you felt you could be rude to
everyone, wondered Tytti.

'Well that's what we're here to find out,'
added Constable Mansikka-aho staring stony-
eyed into the distance. He disliked this woman.
His mind wandered to a game of Sudoku that he
had just started rather badly when the
information about the skull had come in.

Dr Wahlroos pulled out a plastic collection
bag.

'It's through here,' said Kai.

One after the other, they filed along a stark
servants' corridor to a small back door that
opened onto a grassy ditch. Crossing the ditch,
they came to the only oak tree on the property.

An aged tree and its gruesome accessory.

'Well, here we are,' said Anna thinly. 'You can leave through the gardens.' She crossed back over the grassy ditch and firmly closed the door.

Tytti stared at the smooth grey bone of the skull as Dr Wahlroos took several measurements and photographs, an excited Kai trying not to get in the way as he took some himself. Then she plucked it from the tree and dropped it into the plastic bag.

'May I have a closer look?' asked Tytti. 'What's your initial opinion?'

Dr Wahlroos held up the plastic bag so they could all inspect the contents.

'My guess is that it is a young Caucasian male. Perhaps a teenager. I can tell by the wear on the teeth. Also, no wisdom teeth have started to grow yet. See, a fragment of the skull is missing at the back. That might be due to an accident, or attack. I can also see that there has been some demineralisation of the bone by salt water, so this skull may have been in the sea at some point. Nevertheless, there might still be enough DNA for us to make a positive identification. I'll take it back to the lab and do some histology and maybe carbon dating — although the minerals in seawater can sometimes alter the carbon-14 content, and therefore I'd get inaccurate radiocarbon dating results.'

'I'll call you later when more information

comes in,' said Constable Mansikka-aho.

I won't hold my breath, thought Tytti. She walked quickly across the lawn to her bicycle. It was time for her to upend her anonymous critic's estimation of her, and quickly write up the story.

As Tytti left Kai and Dr Wahlroos, she looked up and saw Suvi-Tuuli standing high up on a parapet next to a tower. She went to smile and wave, but then had mixed feelings about it, and stopped. Suvi-Tuuli did not see her. She was standing still, the warm breeze coming in from the sea and ruffling her thin white hair. It would be soothing the arthritis that made the paintbrush harder for her to hold every year. Tytti respected her resilience.

I guess we disturbed her, thought Tytti. Then she wondered for a second. Was now a good time to visit her? She still felt unsettled by the comments Suvi-Tuuli had made regarding her father. What was she supposed to have forgiven him for? But she was probably working on her landscape. Once, Tytti had asked her why this particular painting was so important to her.

'I'm old now and I still haven't created a masterpiece. I find scenery soothing — this corner of the island in particular.' As they stood in her studio, Suvi-Tuuli had lowered her voice in confidence and gestured towards the coastline. 'In summer the pink granite can glisten, torched by a molten sun.' They stood there silently imagining the scene. 'Or the rocks can become butchered twists of steel, in the harsh full moon.' Tytti remembered Suvi-Tuuli's vivid descriptions; she had looked behind her at the painting and seen it through the painter's eyes. No, she would not bother her now. She would wait to visit Suvi-Tuuli.

As she began to cycle back, Tytti sniffed the clear sea air. When she reached the wooden bridge, she stopped her wheels and paused to look over the railing. Many a time she and Kai had played Poohsticks here, dropping a stick into the water and then rushing to the other side of the bridge to see whose stick came through first. She watched her reflection in the water and imagined Kai's face alongside hers, the sea calmly flattening and mirroring all above. Her eyes began to change focus as she stared at the ripples on the water. Now she saw the sea as a living canvas. A living canvas with its own impregnable story underneath.

Chapter Eight

It was five in the evening. Tytti sat at her desk and pondered the day's news. She had nothing better to do and, far less important, a different story to finish. *Missing Lady Found Asleep at Neighbour's House*, typed Tytti, before feeling she had had enough. This story could wait. She still felt the delight of the day before, when she had returned to write the piece on the mystery skull in the tree. She had even managed to squeeze it into that week's edition, something she felt her mystery critic should take note of. But now elation was subsiding, and lesser topics that were begging to be written paled in comparison. Tytti thought that this would be as good a time as ever.

'How would you like to go on a date with Ritva Lempinen?'

Kai looked up from his spreadsheet.

'Here's her picture, in case you've forgotten what she looks like. She's seen you already.' Tytti quickly emailed a highly photoshopped picture of a busty Ritva. 'I'll leave her to tell you more. That's if you'd like to go?'

Tytti lifted her nose a fraction and peered over her computer screen. A slight smile? She thought she had seen one. But then, looking at a picture meant nothing compared to the chemical reaction that could occur when actually meeting a potential lover. Then, you could really tell that each person was attracted to the other. They stood up a bit straighter, breathed in a bit, and a sort of happy-silly look appeared on each of their faces.

'Okay,' said Kai, 'I'll go. What's her telephone number?'

Calling out the digits, Tytti smiled to herself at the thought of how simple it had been. True, the girls Kai had been dating were not really the right types for him, island girls not normally being the most interesting; and Ritva was very experienced in the world of dating. She was sure that Ritva would show Kai a good time. Not that kind of a good time, but a good time nonetheless.

Suddenly, the door crashed open and Teemu stomped in. With a face like thunder, he marched straight into his office and slammed the door. Tytti jumped up to go after him. This was too good to miss! She had never seen him look so red-faced and fuming! She cautiously clicked the door open. Only once had Teemu thrown something at her, but it was best not to take any chances.

'Problem?' Tytti stuck her head around the door. Teemu sat at his desk with his head in his hands. Overall, his appearance was that of one squashed by gravity. One who probably did need a genuine lift. His hair stuck up at all angles where it had been pulled. Tytti thought back to the last thing she knew Teemu had been doing.

'So, how did lunch with your wife go yesterday?'

'She wants a divorce. She's having an affair,' replied Teemu bluntly.

'Your wife is having an affair?' Tytti was truly shocked. She had met Teemu's dull wife, and the thought of her doing anything as reckless as having an affair surprised her.

'No, my housekeeper! Of course it's my bloody wife!'

'Teemu, I am being nice now,' reprimanded Tytti.

'Sorry, it's just, I've only just found out. She told me over coffee at Strindberg! My favourite place! I'll never be able to have coffee there again. Why couldn't she have told me at another coffee shop? The one in the bookshop, for example.' Teemu looked like he was going to cry.

Why indeed, wondered Tytti. Then again, Strindberg did have more exits, and, well…

'I'm sorry Teemu, I really am. Is there anything I can do for you? Run to the off-licence or something?' She could not resist a dig. Despite her sympathetic posturing, she still felt that Teemu in a vulnerable state deserved nothing less.

'No, I'm all set thanks,' said Teemu, too dejected to even rise to the bait. He put his hand in his pocket and drew out a hip flask. He waggled it enticingly at Tytti.

'Join me?'

'Why not.' It was clear that Teemu should not be left alone in this state. 'Whisky Sour please.'

Teemu jumped up and hurried over to a cupboard. Opening it, he exposed a full bar.

'Why don't you tell me all about it,' soothed Tytti. Teemu looked towards her. There was a sadness in his eyes, and his jowls looked deflated. Tytti wondered about his hangdog expression. His anger seemed to have subsided rather quickly. Maybe it had been just for show. Or maybe he was beginning to feel some guilt over the whole debacle. Tytti watched his face as he mixed her drink, and could not help but wonder how much the impending divorce was due to Teemu's drinking.

Chapter Nine

Tytti had decided that today was the day to go
to the castle and confront Anna Tapio. Even if
she was not an arsonist, she was the main person
of interest in all this. She had the most to gain
from the death of Ville Tapio. Plus, she might
have some further information about the skull in
the tree. How had it got there? Yes, maybe it
was time to start acting like a journalist. She had
once heard a film star say that he could only sing
if he *pretended* to sing. Maybe a similar thing
would happen to her if she pretended to be a
proper journalist.

'Let's go into my office.' Tytti, shocked at
hearing Anna be so civil, was caught off guard.
She followed Anna, who was already several
metres ahead, through the entrance doors. The
journey seemed to take only a minute, but it was
a minute filled with a tense silence. Tytti had
seen the charms of Tapiolinna many times
before. She remembered the sound of her
running feet and the laughter from herself and
Kai as they played between the walls. Back then,
the Tapios had lived in this side of the castle, the
hotel side.

They walked on, along a polished wooden
floor that ran the length of a long corridor lined

with paintings and doors. Past rooms with high ceilings, tall windows and distant views of the archipelago. Then the click of Anna's high heels slowed and changed to a clack as she stepped behind a velvet rope and onto a black stone slab. The atmosphere of the house changed immediately. They had arrived on the other side, the medieval side. Here, walls a metre thick contained a smattering of leaded windows. Windows not built for quick access. Anna stopped and unlocked a small door, heavily studded with iron, and ushered Tytti in. Ghostly coats of armour, axes, maces, flails, power-broking tools from another age, hung upon one whitewashed wall. Old pistols and rifles covered the opposite wall. Grim reminders of the violence humans are capable of.

I hope she appreciates my questions, thought Tytti, eyeing the weapons.

How should she start? She could, of course, mention the letter. Maybe it was time to disclose it. Anna walked over to a shining chestnut desk in the middle of the room, which stood on a thickly woven rug.

'Please, sit down, Tytti.'

Sitting down opposite, Tytti began. 'I have a problem with a story I'm working on and I think you might be the only person who can help me. I received a letter the other day, at the castle opening. Look, I have it here with me. It was left in my cardigan pocket in the cloakroom.' She watched Anna closely to see if there was any change in her face at this disclosure. No change; but Anna's right arm shook slightly as she grasped the letter.

Anna read the words out loud: '*"Do you want to solve a murder? Look into the fire".*' Anna sat very still and said nothing. She seemed to be thinking hard.

'A murder,' said Anna, 'but whose?' The letter, more a note really, was not specific.

'I'm guessing, Ville Tapio. The letter says to *"look into the fire"*,' said Tytti. Then she suddenly thought: 'Have you any idea who might want to tip me off?' Maybe finding the author of the letter could be the first step to finding the murderer. Tytti felt suddenly embarrassed by her question. Here she was, asking her distant employer a weird and personal question.

Anna paused.

'I don't know of anybody who would write such a letter. And the only person I can think of who could be considered a murderer would be an arsonist who started the fire. But the police never found out who that person was. That is the only person I can think of.'

Tytti had talked with her father about the fire. Large enough to have been reported on the national news. Maybe her father was right. Anna had had a hard time in the past.

Stay firm, don't get distracted, Tytti told herself.

'But why would a person write a letter rather than just expose the arsonist?' questioned

Anna.

'Maybe they themselves don't know who it is. Do *you* have any idea who this person might be?' Tytti asked probing.

'No, no, of course not. I was also wondering if this person is being serious or not. Maybe it's just a hoax. A hoax devised to upset my new business.'

'Perhaps a disgruntled member of staff or something? Someone seeking to stir up the past,' added Tytti.

Anna hesitated.

'That is, of course, possible; but I treat my staff incredibly well and I don't think I have any enemies there. No, I'm sorry, but I can't help you.'

Tytti was not sure if she believed her. She seemed to be holding back.

'Have you discovered anything more about the skull in the tree?'

Anna looked at Tytti, and there was a coldness in her glance. The aloofness had returned.

'Well, why would I know anything at all about that? I thought that investigation was over.'

'Oh, no. They're going to test for DNA among a few other things.'

'Well, that sounds to me like a waste of time and resources. I'll mention it to the Chief Inspector.' Of course, Anna would have his ear. 'I don't want any trouble associated with the hotel.'

'Well, I doubt the skull will bring disrepute to you. They are only trying to find out who it is.'

'And I don't care why it was put in the tree.' Anna's nostrils flared slightly.

'Do you think it was put there as a threat to you?' suggested Tytti.

Anna gave a deep sigh.

'I can't think of any other reason.' She shuddered. 'All this death makes me uncomfortable.'

'Does it bring back memories?' asked Tytti gently.

Anna looked away.

'Well, yes. The fire at the castle was a terrible time. We were so young. Terhi was only a baby. And Ville Tapio wasn't just my brother-in-law, he was also a close friend. I still miss him.'

'And I imagine your husband, Heike, being drowned the year before...' Tytti stopped abruptly. Anna was looking at her angrily. She had flushed pink.

'Yes, yes, of course. Very much so. Thank goodness for Terhi. I don't know how I'd have made it through those trying times if it hadn't been for her.'

Why is she so angry? Tytti wondered. Well, there didn't seem to be much of a mystery here. Anna seemed to be in the clear. The only thing linking her to the fire was her being in the castle at the time. And why would Anna destroy her own home?

Then Tytti had a thought. 'Have you ever wondered if the arsonist was really trying to kill you?'

'Oh, no. Not at all.'

Chapter Ten

Back at home, stirred up by the interview, Tytti ripped a blank sheet of paper from a pad. So, what did she know so far? The letter. It could have come from anyone with access to the cloakroom, mainly the staff of the party. But would it also have been easy for someone to drop it off? Someone who was there on another pretext? Anna could think of no likely suspect. It was unlikely to be someone in her family. Anna had said it could not be a member of her staff. She had said she treated them well, but Tytti could not imagine Anna treating anybody particularly well. She was off to interview the cloakroom attendant.

'Well, I can't be sure, but I did see a man leave the reception area at one point. I remember him clearly, as he had a German Shepherd dog with him. At first I thought it was Jari, but he would have stopped to say hello. We don't have any guests with dogs staying at the moment, so I thought it a strange thing. We do, of course, get plenty of dog walkers in the area.' The hotel's receptionist, dressed in a grey uniform, tights and high heels, had doubled as the cloakroom attendant for the evening.

'Can you describe him?'

'He was wearing a red baseball cap. That's all I can remember. I was more concerned about the muddy paw prints in the lobby.'

'So it wasn't Jari and his dog.'

'I don't think so. He worked until late into the night. But then, I only saw the back of this man. Sorry. Has there been any more information on the skull? It's all very exciting. Do you think it might be a murder victim?'

'Well, there's no further information as yet,' said Tytti sombrely.

'Excuse me a moment.' The telephone in the office had rung. As the receptionist left, Tytti had an idea.

She did not feel guilt as such for stealing the book, as she knew that thievery, in this case, was a means to an end and not motivated by the thrill of deceit, or lack of funds, or whatever else it was that prompted thieves to steal. (She did, however, commend herself on how easy it had been.) And the others? One book had been easily dusted off after being left on her windowsill; but it had taken Tytti a while to uncover the box that had been stored away in the attic and to find the other one.

The letter lay on her table. A magnifying glass was in her hand. The letter, a bit crumpled now from its time in Tytti's pocket, was still clearly legible and provocative. Now it was time to see if the three guest books stacked on her desk would reveal anything.

The first book, which she had taken from the hotel reception desk, had an inaugural entry from only a week ago, when the castle had first opened as a hotel. On the night the letter had been dropped off there were maybe twenty entries. Many of the guests had been friends of the Tapio family who had sailed in on their yachts especially to support Anna.

With a feeling of excitement, Tytti began to study the names of those who had registered at the hotel. An A here, an E there—she soon saw that none of the letters in the first entry matched the handwriting of the mystery note. Reading down the list, she noticed several famous names, but still no character of the alphabet that matched those of the tip-off note. Well, this book had been a long shot anyway. She still had her own dusty guest book and her mother's old visitors' book to investigate.

Her mother had been a friendly soul and had invited many islanders over for coffee and cake. Her mother's old visitors' book should just about cover the older generation, and her guest book might have a few droll comments in it from the younger cohort. Tytti did after all live by the sea. Next to a shallow bay, perfect for swimming. A place which, in the summer, had islanders knocking on her door with offerings of cake while surreptitiously hiding their swimming costumes.

Tytti read through her own and then her

mother's visitors' book. By the time she had reached the end, the elation of the hunt had subsided and turned to disillusionment. Despite rushes of exhilaration as this or that letter began to look the same, when examined more closely with the magnifying glass, not one of them matched.

With a sore neck from poring over the books, Tytti finally admitted to herself that no character of the alphabet in any of the three books matched any character in the tip-off note. In frustration, she slammed the last book shut and pushed it away across the table. She had hoped beyond hope that she would detect a match, and the person who had tipped her off would be exposed as one of the islanders. Not that any of them seemed malevolent, but one could never tell.

Then she started. Her mother's visitors' book lay closed on the table. As she pulled it closer, something caught her eye. It was her mother's handwriting.

Chapter Eleven

Tytti had waited until late evening, when the castle reception was empty, and slipped the guest book back.

Now, the following morning, it was a sunny day, and rather than go to the office she felt she would be better employed in her sleuthing. She was wondering whether Jari the security guard would be able to tell her anything about the skull.

As she arrived on her bicycle at his home on the other side of the island, Jari was sitting on a white plastic chair in the garden with the sun beating down on his bald head. He had on a red and blue checked shirt and navy and grey checked knee-length shorts that were held up quite high around his waist with black braces. He had white sports socks on and a pair of green rubber shoes. He had once been shot in the thigh during a jewellery heist gone wrong on the mainland, and he had a stick that he rarely used. He got up as he saw Tytti pull in to his driveway.

'Hello there,' he said happily. The island was full of happy people.

'Hello, Jari. Do you have a minute? I'd like to ask you some questions for an, er, article.' She had forgotten that she might need a cover story.

'Sure, sure. Would you like a beer?'

'Yes, please,' replied Tytti. She felt hot and dusty from the long bicycle ride. Jari strained as he leant over and plucked another beer can from the cooler.

'What is this article about?' asked Jari, passing the beer over to Tytti. He gestured to her to pull up a chair.

'The hotel opening last week.' Tytti cracked open the beer, a traditional Finnish beer, in a small can. 'I was wondering why you were hired to do security?'

Jari looked at Tytti sideways. He had, of course, once been a detective.

'Well, Anna Tapio called me in as she'd been receiving threats.'

Tytti choked on her beer. Why had Anna not told *her* that?

'Threats from whom?'

'That's the thing. She said she had no idea. She said it was a small thing and she didn't feel the need to report it to the police, but the threats had mentioned the party.'

'Do you have any idea who might have tried to threaten her?' Tytti paused. 'How was she threatened?'

'Somebody left her several handwritten notes. Obviously this person has no fear of their handwriting being matched. Or their fingerprints — although they could have been wearing latex gloves when they wrote it. It hasn't been deemed necessary to check for such things, as no crime has been committed.'

Tytti sipped her beer and pondered. Jari's use of the term 'latex gloves' made the threat sound somehow more sinister.

'I saw you at the party. When did your dog sniff out the skull?'

'After the event, I let him off his leash to have a run around. Gunnar used to be a cadaver dog in Helsinki before he retired and came to me.'

'Do you have any idea who might have put the skull in the tree?'

Jari paused to consider the question.

'Sorry, no... Wait, she left the threatening notes with me.' Jari placed his beer on the white plastic table and went inside. The mesh door to keep the mosquitoes out swung loosely as he passed through. 'Help yourself to another beer,' he called. The beer can contained only 33 cl.

Jari returned with three pages of squared paper that looked as though they had been ripped out of a notebook.

'What do you think of this?' said Tytti, passing across the letter that had been left in her cardigan. She took a gulp of her beer. Jari raised his eyebrows as he read the letter, then let out a low whistle.

'I'd say they were all written by members of the same family. I think this one here — your one,' Jari held up the letter, 'was written by a man. The writing is larger, stronger. Whereas the letters Anna gave me are written in a smaller, neater script.'

'Do you know of anyone else on the island who has a German Shepherd dog?' asked Tytti. Jari looked surprised.

'Well, yes, now you mention it. There was a man in the dog park with one the other day. He arrived just as we were leaving. He said his dog wasn't very friendly so he came to the dog park late in the evening when all the other dogs had left. Why do you ask?'

But Tytti was not listening. Could it be…? she thought.

Chapter Twelve

During the night, the clouds in the sky had amassed and a dark north-easterly wind had galloped in. Still in a sleepy haze, Tytti woke to hear the first cloudburst spatter against her window. Rolling onto her back and with half-closed eyes, she squinted up at the icon of Ukko, God of Thunder, nailed to the wall, and silently cursed him for raising a storm. Her washing was out.

The icon had been passed down with the house by her predecessors, from a time when Finland had been more swamp than land. Tytti felt safe in the old house: its sounds, the creaks and groans, made her feel connected to her ancestors, who would have heard the same. Nobody knew exactly when the house was built. It had come Tytti's way when her late grandmother had willed it to her. Made of logs that had been left unpainted and had now weathered to a soft silvery grey, it had a twisted pitched roof (now safe from leaks, thanks to her grandad's repairs) and leaded panes of glass in its four small windows. It was long, low and perfectly symmetrical in a crooked kind of way. There was a room for living to the left and a pantry and sauna to the right — half and half.

But being such an old house, it was always cold.

Wrapping herself in a blanket, Tytti pulled herself from her bed and went to look at the inside thermometer. Only 18 degrees! Her phone rang.

'It's Denis. What time shall we meet?' Tytti's heart sank. She had forgotten that she had agreed to go on a dig with Denis that day.

While diligently cleaning the office one morning, Denis the cleaner had noticed a small silver object holding down a pile of papers on Kai's desk. On closer inspection, he had suspected that the unusual paperweight might actually be a silver bar that may have come from some kind of ancient hoard. Holding back his excitement, Denis had patiently waited for Kai to arrive, using the free hour he had to clean the slats of the blinds, and then, after a hurried introduction, launched straight into asking Kai where it had come from. Tytti had arrived just as Kai had been describing the area where his godfather, Ulrich, had discovered the bar before it was given to him as a little boy. At the time, Ulrich and he had searched the area together and come up with nothing, so they guessed it might have been dropped by some kind of trader travelling through. Tytti had sensed what was coming. She had heard the excitement in Denis's voice. An excitement she had only ever heard once before, back during one summer when he had worked on a dig in the field next to her father's graveyard. She felt the question coming: the request for her to spend a day digging around in the dirt. At the time, Tytti had not felt particularly enthused about the idea, and was even less so now that the day had begun cold, wet and windy. But there was something about Denis that made her feel that she did not want to let him down. He was shy and quiet and, like most reserved people, his feelings became easily bruised if handled incorrectly. If she chose not to go, she could imagine him sitting there digging alone, feeling sad because she had chosen not to join him. Maybe even crying into the dirt as he wondered what he had done to offend her. No, she would not let him down.

'I'll meet you at the castle stables in an hour then.'

Tytti had begun to grow impatient as she stood waiting at the stables for a late Denis. In five more minutes, he would be fifteen whole minutes late! Tytti thought fifteen minutes above and beyond a reasonable time to wait for someone to turn up. As she stood sheltering in the doorway of the barn, she was starting to have thoughts of going back to her comparatively warm house when a horse and rider appeared, dripping wet and spattered with mud. Knowing a bit about horses and thinking it polite to do so, Tytti lightly took the reins to prevent the horse from walking off as the oilskin-clad rider went to dismount.

'Hi,' said Tytti.

'Hi,' said the hooded figure. 'It's Tytti, isn't it?'

Tytti was taken aback by what sounded like a girl knowing who she was.

'Yes.' Hazarding a guess, Tytti went on: 'Since you know who I am, is that you Annika Tapio?'

Annika pulled back her hood and laughed.

'Yes! Gosh, you're good. Kai mentioned that you were a very good journalist.'

Tytti felt herself redden to hear of her reputation.

'My brother said you'd be over today. Looking for silver?'

'Hmm, well, when you put it like that... My friend Denis is interested in that kind of thing.'

'Your boyfriend?'

'Er, no, Denis is just a friend.' Tytti looked more closely at Annika and remembered that she must be around fourteen, an acceptable age to be so interested in boyfriends. They went into the barn and Tytti watched the teenager idly, as she undid several leather straps to remove the saddle and bridle. Fed up now, she cursed Denis inwardly for making her be there, and hunted for a topic for conversation.

'Do you happen to know where your brother is?'

'He's gone out... On a date!'

A date? thought Tytti. Who could he be on a date with at this time? She had only just given

Ritva's phone number to him, and Ritva would definitely have told her if he had called. In her mind, Tytti ran through a list of likely females who resided on the island. Yet more talk about dating! Without wanting to, she remembered a rather unpleasant lunch she had had involving two of her friends, their other halves and her single self. The couples had sat there being judgemental and openly discussing between themselves how Tytti might try speed dating as a final and desperate attempt to meet a man. They had been utterly unable to fathom an existence without a mate, and had looked down on Tytti as rather a poor specimen for being twenty-five and single. Needless to say, that had been the last lunch they had shared together, and the close friendships she had had with these two important people had fizzled out.

Denis's late arrival had been caused by too much enthusiasm. He had been packing up all manner of trowels, spoons, brushes and sieves before he noticed that time was flying by.

'I'm so sorry, Tytti,' he said, still shaking a little from the cold and the trauma of his maniacal moped ride. 'I thought I'd bring some equipment in case we get lucky.'

Denis pulled a map from his waterproof jacket and began to work out the direction they must take to find the location where the bar had been discovered. Tytti looked on in annoyance: she clearly remembered hearing Kai tell Denis that it was round the back of the stables and across a few fields. But she knew enough about the combination of men and maps not to mention it. She had also heard Kai tell Denis that nature had rather taken over the spot and that he was not sure what they might find there.

'Kai said the area is now pretty much a thicket, so we may have to scramble through some undergrowth to look for stuff,' said Denis, giving Tytti a heads-up. 'Sorry about that.'

'No problem at all,' lied Tytti.

And that's why I like you, thought Denis, smiling to himself. You just get on with it.

Climbing over a wooden fence, they began to walk through the first horse field, trying as much as possible to avoid the muddy patches where a Wellington boot could be lost. The closer they came to the sea, the stronger the wind blew, delaying their arrival.

'Nearly there,' called Denis, the wind pinning his blue nylon cagoule to his thin frame.

An icy finger of wind wound itself inside Tytti's ear, already ringing from the rain. They were approaching the coppice, a tangle of tree, bramble and fern. A place where summer berries dwindled. The noise was deafening now as the wind boomed straight from the sea. Denis headed in first using an old ski pole to smack away the undergrowth. Shielded by the trees, the wind became a disturbing moan.

'Be careful,' shouted Denis.

Tytti's feet snagged on roots and skidded

across mossy rocks. Where the undergrowth
cleared, the ground was soft with humus and
pine needles, the only sound, bar the wind,
coming from a fir cone being kicked or crunched
underfoot. Tytti brushed past bracken and
stepped over rotting tree trunks that littered the
ground.

'Let's stop here and start to look around,'
yelled Denis, halting.

Tytti picked up a long stick and started to
poke around in the undergrowth. When she
happened upon an object of a similar size to the
silver bar, she picked it up with a chilled hand
and inspected it. No, it was just a rock.

After one hour of searching, she began to
think that it was a hopeless task and sat down to
rest on a wet boulder. She had not found
anything else of a similar size and weight to the
silver paperweight. Maybe she was looking for
the wrong thing. They had reached the footpath
that ran around the edge of the island. The sea
was beating the rocks below, and a squabble of
seagulls was being pushed back with every
squall. Denis stood at the edge of the granite
clifftop. There was nowhere left to search.

Denis had just pulled away on his moped, with a
borrowed stable bucket on his lap containing
some nonetheless potentially interesting rocks,
when Tytti saw Kai's car draw up. Kai opened
the window.

'So, how did the date go?' Tytti launched in,

standing there with her wind-blown hair full of forest detritus, and spots of mud on her face.

'Er, fine, thank you.' He went quiet. He was not one to talk about matters of the heart. Or at least not to Tytti. 'Would you like to come up to the castle and clean up a bit before you go? You could wait until the storm died down before you cycled home.'

Unaware of quite how she looked, Tytti jumped into Kai's immaculate Range Rover.

'Not really a day for excavating,' said Kai, a faint smile on his face as he noted Tytti's bedraggled appearance.

'Not really, but I didn't want to let Denis down. He does love to dig. Did he ever tell you why he works as a cleaner? He's been looking after his sick mother since he was twelve. She has emphysema and needs help with her breathing equipment most of the time. He wanted a job where he could just work for a few hours, so he could be with her, as she's housebound.'

'I'm sorry to hear that. He's a good bloke, that Denis. He said he would love to study archaeology one day.'

I knew it! thought Tytti heatedly. He does want to go to university, and he is playing down his responsibility to his mother. I must find a way to help him.

Tytti was surprised at her own response. For some reason, she felt it her duty to help Denis out of his predicament. Help him get to university somehow.

As they pulled up at the castle, a taxi was pulling away and a woman, her bobbed hair drenched by the rain, was standing at the door with several suitcases. Kai leaned forward and peered through the wet windscreen.

'I think that's Terhi. She's been working in London, so why she's here I do not know.'

Kai raked up the handbrake and turned off the engine.

Chapter Thirteen

Terhi was tired. She had spent seventy-two hours without sleep, working on a report for an investment banking client, sending her minions running around the building to deliver new pages to a variety of higher-up people for review while she sat with the lawyers, on the phone to the client, balancing what they could and could not get away with. The smell of Pad Thai and coffee grounds lingered in the room, but the building's security system did not allow for open windows — unless a bomb went off or there was a fire, in which case they would all spring open, encouraging you to jump. She had finally finished checking the important page of pipelines at about 5 a.m. The document had been full of errors, but the correct legal disclaimer had been included. She hoped the client did not read it. It was more of a souvenir really.

Terhi gave a grim laugh as she stared out of her London office window directly into the tinted glass-faced window opposite. The City was tiny. All those beautiful narrow mediaeval streets planted with oafish glass-and-steel office blocks. Anyway, she would be out of it soon. She had worked so hard to outperform the City boys, and now she had to leave. She could say she'd got a better offer somewhere else, but banking was a small world and they would soon find out that she had lied. Her rule had always been "never at work". It was the quickest way for them to lose respect for you. What a lonely fool she had been to give in to him.

A wave of sickness made her reach for the dustbin. Oh, to hell with it. She hit the spacebar, bringing her computer back to life.

> *'John, I am sorry to say that I am giving notice due to a family emergency which means I have to return to Finland immediately. As I haven't taken a day off in four years, I think I have enough holiday leave due to waive my notice period and leave tomorrow. Goodbye, Terhi.'*

She hit send, stood up and reached for her coat.

John sat at the restaurant table with his wife and their friends. His Blackberry buzzed in his pocket, so he excused himself and went to read the message in the loo. The glamorous world of banking. At least now he was a Head he didn't have to kip under his desk anymore: he had underlings to do that. That Terhi had been the most promising of the lot, but she'd been slacking for the last few weeks. Time he gave her a verbal lashing. Or maybe if he shagged her again, she would perk up?

Chapter Fourteen

'Terhi! How are you?' said Kai, hugging his sister. 'And what are you doing here? I thought you were still tied up in that oil and gas deal, the one that horrible MP keeps claiming there are no British interests in.'

'I was, I am, but, oh, Kai... I'm pregnant, and John, my boss, he's the father.' Terhi choked back her tears.

'But that's good news, right? You're going to be okay, right? The baby's okay, isn't it?'

'Yes, the baby's going to be fine, but...'

'Then nothing else matters,' interjected Kai. 'That part is over. You're home now and everything's going to be okay.' For once Kai's timing was spot on.

Tytti stood by in admiration, watching the warmth between brother and sister as Kai took hold of the situation. Kai was a good brother and a good man; she could see that.

'Let's all go and have some coffee and a catch up. Tytti and I have got something very exciting to tell you about.'

In the mirror of a lavish marble bathroom, Tytti viewed herself in despair. She wore a faded cotton summer dress tucked into dirty brown gardening trousers; the only dry clothes left after the morning rain soaked her washing. All she could do was pick the leaves from her hair and wipe the mud from her face. Walking out into the corridor, she could hear voices coming from a room across the hall. She went in and sat down, slowly sinking onto a gold-fringed, red velvet sofa and back into its bright-green silk cushions. Her eyes travelled over the tiled walls with their brightly painted Ottoman tulips.

'You know it was never our choice. Mother was so determined for us to become bankers that we never stood a chance.' Terhi was standing by the window. 'Have you seen her recently? I think she's become even worse. I always feel that I owe an explanation for her.' She smiled. 'Sorry about all the drama. I'm feeling a bit saner now.'

'So how long do you have before your baby is born?'

'Oh, ages yet. There's plenty of time to get on my feet again.'

'Oh, no, you'll be staying right off those feet, if I have anything to do with it,' said Kai.

The housekeeper arrived with the most glamorous coffee set Tytti had ever seen.

'I didn't know you were a banker before. I thought you were a trader.'

'Yes, you're right. I was a trader. And, well... it's not something I wish to get around. It can attract quite the wrong type of... girl.' Kai blushed. Terhi caught Tytti's eye and they both smiled.

Since he had arrived back on the island, Tytti had seen how awkward Kai felt about his recent life. How he preferred to bypass it in conversation and instead reminisce back to his years spent growing up at the castle. Tytti remembered their favourite game — charging around as Knights of the Realm with wooden swords and tea-towel capes. Tytti had obstinately refused to play the damsel in distress, preferring the role of mounted warrior. Back then, all Kai had wanted to do was save the kingdom. But then came university, and then the job in Stockholm. Tytti remembered him telling her how shocked he had been when he started work. The vileness of the people. She remembered him vowing that he would never become like them. And he seemed to have stayed true to his vow, to a point. He had not saved the kingdom, but people's goodwill had kept him sane and she was proud to think that he had stayed strong and always treated his fellow employees well, unlike many of his colleagues, who felt that they could pass down the abuses of their seniors. Those were the weak ones. All City money was about was the ongoing survival of the world's richest in splendour, and Kai considered such money to have no meaning. A pound to a beggar. Now that was a fortune. It was a fine position to take for a man with his silver-spoon background.

'Terhi!' A little boy flew across the room,

grabbed her, and planted a big wet kiss on her face. Then, grabbing her hand in a firm little grip, he ordered: 'Come play.'

'And here comes my terrible little brother JoJo,' said Kai, darting out of the way as JoJo tried to punch him. It seemed that JoJo had just appointed himself Terhi's new boss.

Chapter Fifteen

The next day, Tytti was back in the office. Shoes off, she sat with her long legs stretched out on the little red sofa, enjoying the lull after another completed weekly edition. A legitimate time to take an honest rest. This edition had headlined with a story about a 'suspected fire' at a school. The fire brigade had been called to the scene only to discover two tramps grilling sausages. Meanwhile Kai had pushed off on another lunch date, although this time Tytti did not mind being left alone.

Kai was fitting in well. Still kind, thoughtful and funny, he still made her laugh — pulling faces behind Teemu's back. Pinging the odd rubber band. And since he had arrived there was a sense of excitement about the place. Tytti now felt that anything was possible; she just had to get up and do it. After years of sitting in her office chair waiting for things to happen, she finally felt that she could have the work life she had dreamed about when she first started all those years ago. Since the letter had arrived, she had felt inspired to act like a real journalist. Chasing down stories and not waiting for the phone to ring. She felt active, ready for anything. She had even adjusted the many knobs and levers of her plastic office chair in order to sit up a little straighter. After years of slouching — almost hiding under her desk — she knew that this lifting of spirits was due to the presence of Kai. She could also see him slightly better. Teemu came in.

'Good-oh. Everything finished? Shall we pop over to Strindberg for drinks? Be a nice way to end the edition.'

Tytti wrinkled her nose at the thought. Teemu was hardly bearable in the office. And she had spent more time than she felt strictly necessary consoling him recently. No, she had had her dose of Teemu for the time being.

'No thanks. And since when do we celebrate putting an edition to bed? Plus Kai isn't here to join the festivities.'

Teemu frowned at the thought of Kai coming along. He wanted to get Tytti on her own. He felt he had something to tell her. Something that had been brewing for a while. Tytti had been supportive to him since his wife's emancipation, and Teemu felt they had become closer. He had always wondered if their banter might connote something deeper. Something, well, more lustful. And Kai was out of the office just now; maybe this was the only chance he would get.

Teemu went over to the little red sofa and put his hand on Tytti's leg.

Tytti pushed his hand away, thinking he wanted her to move her legs to make space for him to sit down. She had no idea that he had just made a pass at her.

Teemu withdrew nervously. Had she slapped his hand away in a playful way? Should he make another attempt? He had rather a silly look on his face.

Having declined Teemu's invitation, Tytti thought she might wander over to Ritva's to see if Kai had phoned yet. What was taking him so long? She felt embarrassed to ask him directly: it might seem like she was being pushy.

The sun was shining that day and the market was busy. The tourist boat had just been, and Americans, Chinese, English — tourists of all sorts — were wandering like ants with shopping bags around the market stalls. The market had swollen: the everyday stalls bearing trays of brightly coloured berries and neatly stacked vegetables had been joined by stalls selling reindeer goods, wooden sculptures, ceramic jewellery, all kinds of tourist tat. (But high-quality, expensive tourist tat, as this was after all Finland, winner of a host of "Best of" awards, including the not so welcome title, "Most Expensive in Europe".)

Tytti closed the office door and walked across the market square past wrinkled old ladies knitting woolly hats, their beady eyes flitting around the market's bustling activity. The sharp smell of oily fish from the fishing boats moored next to the market square met

Tytti's nostrils, overpowered only by the heady scent of strawberries brought in by locals to sell that day from folding tables. And now the scents of cardamom and coffee wafting from the book shop café.

Ritva was sitting on a bench outside, an open book resting face down on her knee. Tytti sat down next to her. Lili, Ritva's little Shih Tzu, got up from her patch in the sun to say hello.

'How are you today?'

'So-so, thank you. How are you?'

'Quite well, thank you. Has Kai phoned yet?'

Ritva started in her seat.

'You gave him my phone number?'

'Well, yes, of course. You said you liked him, so I gave him your number. He said he'd call you for a date.' Tytti had many qualities, but tact was not one of them. She watched as Ritva, almost imperceptibly, cringed. Maybe Kai knowing that Ritva liked him was not a good thing. Had she been wrong to give him Ritva's number? It almost made it seem like she was introducing two beasts for mating, rather than gentler pleasures. She could see that Ritva felt that way.

'Well, thank you for doing that,' said Ritva. 'When did you give him my phone number? He hasn't called yet.'

'Not long ago, actually — not long at all. He'll call you today, I'm sure of it.'

Ritva's stomach curdled. Unwittingly, Tytti

had put her nerves on high alert.

Suddenly, Ritva panicked.

'But what should I say? Where should we go?'

'Say hello and invite him over here for coffee.'

'Did you show him my picture?'

Tytti nodded.

'Which picture did you show him?' added Ritva more sternly.

'Your dating profile one. The one you asked me to, er, "tidy up".' Deftly changing the subject, Tytti asked, 'Has the book I asked you to order arrived yet?' Not wanting to alert Ritva to the letter, she quickly added, 'So I can write that article, on, er, crime.'

'Sure, sure. It's inside, under the counter. Help yourself.' Distracted, Ritva peered over at the *Tapiolinna Times* office. Was Kai in there reaching for his phone? Should she go over there — and say what? Annoyed for a second, Ritva wished Tytti had given her *his* number, so she was in control. Then sitting back, she decided to continue enjoying the sunshine with Lili, daydreaming about Kai rather than thinking about moving.

To avoid any nosiness on Ritva's part, Tytti sank down as low as possible into one of the bookshop's squashy brown leather chairs. (Occasionally these chairs proved so yielding that a customer had been known to fall asleep for several hours, book in hand, after browsing for a potential purchase. Ritva would let them sleep, as they usually bought the book out of embarrassment in the end.)

Flicking through the tome, Tytti came to the chapter she needed, and began to read:

"Handwriting is a mixture of both nature and nurture. Penmanship is shaped by how people are taught to write. However, genetics also play a role in shaping how a person dots their i's and crosses their t's."

Jari had observed that the author of the threatening letters was probably related to the writer of the tip-off note. Maybe genetics had played a role? Thinking she would read more later, Tytti returned to the office with the book under her arm. As she arrived, she saw that Kai was sitting on the little red sofa with a set of colour photos spread across the coffee table. He was holding one up and scrutinising it.

'Hey, Tytti, come and look at this. I've found something odd about the skull in the tree. These are the pictures I took. I used a macro setting for a few of them. I was just trying out the camera really. Look at these marks on the skull.'

Tytti went and hovered over the table next to Kai. She took the photo Kai was holding and inspected it.

'What do you mean? I can't see anything.'

'Look more closely. See, under the eye sockets? It looks like there's a small hole under each one.'

Tytti looked again. Kai was right. The holes were tiny, almost indiscernible.

I wonder what Dr Wahlroos has made of these, thought Tytti.

'What do you think they could be?' asked Kai.

'I've no idea.' Tytti picked up another photograph. Looking closely at it, she noticed the angle. She could just see the small figure of Suvi-Tuuli at the top of the picture. Then she had an idea. But first, she wanted answers from her father.

Perched on the edge of a worn armchair in the sitting room of the vicarage, Tytti watched her father sweep out the ashes from the fireplace.

'Dad, I was speaking with Suvi-Tuuli the other day, and she alluded to a secret that you've kept from me.' Her father did not turn around and continued to sweep. 'She asked me if I had forgiven you but didn't disclose what for. What was she talking about?' There was a thud from the kitchen. Tytti looked at her father to see if he knew what the thump was. Her father had frozen.

Before he could stop her, Tytti had dashed from her chair and opened the kitchen door. In the dim light she could just make out a smartly dressed woman bending over. She was picking a potato off the floor.

Tytti stared at the woman and tried to place

her face.

'Tytti, this is Miina.' Her father had followed her into the kitchen.

The woman was unfamiliar to Tytti. She put out a hand and they shook.

'She's here to drop off some money for the collection.'

So why is she holding a potato? thought Tytti. She looked down at the table, at a pile of potatoes that had already been peeled.

'Er… and, yes, well, I invited her to stay for dinner.'

So why on earth is she preparing it? thought Tytti. Something was up.

'Are you a chef? What is it you do?' Tytti probed.

'Er, well…' The woman was visibly thrown by Tytti's directness. 'I'm a consultant. My office is currently in Helsinki, but I plan to move to the island.'

She had clearly made the woman feel uncomfortable. Maybe it was time to win her over. But then why had her father said that the woman was only there to drop off money? Risto smiled unwisely. He actually felt some relief at Tytti finally meeting Miina. He didn't like to keep important things from her, and Miina was becoming just that. And Tytti was open-minded enough (although more than a little opinionated). But should he tell her why they had been using the dropping off of collection money as a cover? No. Now was not the time.

Chapter Sixteen

The sound of the siren faded into the distance as the ambulance sped away. Tytti was left standing at the front door of the castle with Annika and JoJo. Kai's panicky phone call had brought her rushing over. Terhi had begun to feel ill early that morning — a problem at any time, but especially since her pregnancy was only eight weeks along. The nanny was on her day off and Anna was in Stockholm, so Kai had decided that Tytti must be called. Tytti felt proud that Kai trusted her enough to look after his siblings while he was at the hospital with Terhi.

'Don't worry about your sister; she's going to be fine. This always happens to pregnant women,' fibbed Tytti. JoJo looked up at her, his little face worried.

'That's right,' continued Annika, 'It happens all the time.'

The little boy thought about it for a moment and his face relaxed a little. He adored his aunt and was glad to hear the white lie.

'What do you want to do?' deflected Tytti.

'Swim!' yelled JoJo, grabbing Tytti's hand and pulling her towards the sea. 'I'm going to beat you both at swimming!'

'I don't think so,' said Annika, 'not yet anyway. Show me your foot.' JoJo stuck out his leg. 'Hmm, your feet are growing nicely, but you're going to need nice long flipper feet to beat us!'

Half-listening to their chitter-chatter, Tytti and the children began walking along the footbridge to the bathhouse. The simple nailed planks of faded grey wood, worn by decades of damp footprints and dripping seawater, stretched out before them. An extravagant structure, the bathhouse had four fat, ornate columns and curved wooden railings of white, and a black, elaborately tiled roof. On the far side a ladder took you down into the water. Water that today was warm and sandy as it stirred under a hazy blue sky.

As the children changed into bathing costumes, a thought crossed Tytti's mind. Where was their father, Simo? Why had Kai not called him? As things seemed to have calmed down and JoJo was happily splashing in the water, Tytti decided to raise the subject with Annika.

'So, where's your father today?'

'At home.' Annika gestured towards a small island covered in fir trees in the distance. 'Kai and he haven't been getting along. They do try to be civil in front of JoJo and me, but they always end up fighting. That must be why he called you instead of dad. He trusts you. Plus dad isn't the best person to deal with in an emergency. He's a poet, you know. He has an artistic temperament; he'd probably just add to the panic.' Annika laughed. 'I'm glad you're here.'

Tytti blushed inwardly at the honest, childish praise.

The whirring of propeller blades coming in from the horizon made them all look up. They waited, staring, until they saw a black helicopter flying in directly towards them like a colossal mosquito homing in to bite. The whirring turned to thumping as the helicopter drew nearer. Sticking a defensive finger into each ear, and with baleful eyes, Tytti watched the shiny machine rotate a slow quarter-circle and land. As the engine cut off and the propeller slowed, a border of hollyhocks lay smacked at an angle from the hard blast of air.

'Mum's back. She'll be able to look after JoJo now. I'm off to Dad's,' grinned Annika, knowing when to make a swift exit. JoJo was now playing with his trucks in the sand.

Still chatting, Tytti and Annika walked to the end of a nearby jetty where a small wooden rowboat floated. Tytti sat down and dropped her feet into the lukewarm water. Annika reached across and untied the mooring rope. With a dull thud, it landed in the bottom of the boat, and the vessel drifted free for a moment. iPhone in hand, Annika put one foot into the boat and, doing a temporary split, pushed off from the jetty with the other. Wobbling and twisting to keep her balance, she finally sat down and grabbed the oars. Tytti watched, holding her breath. Annika was a young free spirit and she wasn't going to correct her methods, however perilous they might be.

As the sound of oars on water faded, Tytti listened to the occasional taps and bangs of the jetty as it jiggled against the sea. She leaned back and gazed up at a cloudless sky. Somewhere among the endless rigmarole of work, summer had arrived.

Poised and shoeless, Tytti crossed the cool lawn, towards the helicopter. Ulrich Tollet, a tall grey-haired man of about fifty, stood with Anna. She nodded hello to Ulrich as Anna dealt with a sandy JoJo, brushing him down rather harshly while trying not to get sand on herself. Ulrich barely nodded back. He seemed to feel no need to make small talk.

Maybe he thinks me beyond conversation somehow, thought Tytti. No, he probably just has things on his mind. Grand things to do with money and gold. Ulrich ran an investment bank in Stockholm, the one where Kai had been working. He was known to be standoffish and was unpopular with the islanders due to the way he carried himself. As if he owned the sunlight.

I must stop being so judgemental, reprimanded Tytti. But she had only the merest shadow of a doubt that she had been right first time.

Tytti was thankful that Kai had phoned his mother beforehand to explain the situation.

'Thank you, Tytti,' Anna said, 'for helping with the children.' Tytti wondered if Anna would ask her anything about the investigation into the letter. She wondered if Ulrich knew about the situation. It was perhaps best not to broach the subject in case he was not party to it. She also wanted to ask how Terhi was doing at the hospital, but thought it best not to raise the issue in front of JoJo. Anna herself was making no move to go there, so she guessed things must be in hand.

'Do you have a moment to talk?' asked Tytti under her breath.

'Of course,' replied Anna. 'Ulrich can look after JoJo.' Ulrich pursed his lips in a gesture of annoyance as they turned and began to walk away. Waiting until they were out of earshot, Tytti began: 'Why didn't you mention the threats *you* had received when I told you about the letter *I* had received?' Anna looked up at her in surprise. And Tytti noted a hint of fear there too. They began to walk across the lawn and down to the sea.

'I didn't feel them to be relevant at the time.'

'How come? They could have come from the same source as the letter that was left in my pocket. They could have been a clue.'

'How do you know about them anyway?'

'Jari showed them to me. I went to see him

to check if he had seen anything suspicious on the evening of the hotel opening. The night the skull was left. Why was he guarding the bay area?'

'No real reason.'

'Was it in case of a boat arriving?'

'I suppose so.' An awkward silence fell as they continued to walk down to the seashore. As they progressed, the grass became crunchy underfoot. It was the kind of grass that only grew by the sea, surviving by adapting to become salted and tough. Before Tytti could continue her line of reasoning, Anna asked, 'Why are you investigating the skull when you should be investigating who the letter came from?'

'The skull in the tree is still a story I should be exploring for the newspaper.' The new edition with the story was to come out the next morning.

For once, I was doing some work, thought Tytti in annoyance. Anna gazed off into the distance.

'Well, I'm not sure you should waste your time investigating that,' said Anna. She continued in an offhand manner: 'Have you told anybody about the letters?'

'No.'

'You see, I don't want it getting out. I don't want anything to upset business at the hotel. You would only be causing trouble if others became aware of the situation.' There was a long pause. 'I wouldn't want to have to stop you.'

Tytti was startled at the unveiled threat.

'Stop me?'

'Well, let's not worry about that for the time being. I'm sure you know to do the right thing.'

Chapter Seventeen

Tytti peeled the fluorescent yellow sticky note away from her screen. 'Meeting at ten,' it read. What had she done now? As it was almost ten-thirty, she pushed open Teemu's office door to see if anyone was still gathered there. She was met by two stony faces. The dregs of two cups of coffee sat on the meeting table. Next to them, a copy of the *Tapiolinna Times*. The edition that had come out that morning.

'Here at last,' said Teemu snidely, implying that Tytti was rarely, if ever, in the office on time. He had felt rejected by Tytti, the day he had made his unnoticed pass at her. Now it was time for payback.

This must be serious, thought Tytti. Anna is with him.

It was the first time Tytti had ever seen Anna inside her office. Yes — *her* office. Anna was ultimately her true employer.

'As you're finally here, take a seat,' ordered Teemu.

'I'd rather stand,' objected Tytti.

'Well, whatever you like. You're still fired,' said Anna calmly. She was sitting in the sunshine on the window seat.

'Well, not exactly *fired*, Anna, but I will have

to suspend her.'

'For what?!'

'I think you know for what,' smirked Anna.

'I don't. For what?'

'For what—for what?!' Teemu snapped. He picked up the newspaper and waved it in Tytti's face. 'For writing a sensational article on a skull being found at the castle!'

'Yes, I wrote the article. I am a journalist!'

'But did you ever think to get up out of your chair to do any research?' asked Anna.

'You didn't have enough information to write the piece. You should have waited!' said Teemu angrily, catching his stride. 'You printed facts that hadn't been confirmed and you made it sound as if there might be an unknown culprit. You mentioned the forensics as if it was a murder case.'

And you, as editor, should have checked the edition and pulled the piece, thought Tytti as she gritted her teeth. But she was not one to drop another in it. Anyway, she was not in that much trouble. Anna would not after all sue her own newspaper.

'Suspended?' Tytti said, looking helplessly at Teemu for assistance that was not forthcoming. 'For how long?'

'One—'

'Well, whether you are suspended or fired depends on your attitude,' Anna resumed.

That's not what we agreed on, thought Teemu.

'So, if Tytti works on her attitude, she can have her job back.'

Teemu stood blinking incredulously. Tytti slumped somewhat. There it was. Her "retirement," suggested in the letter of complaint, had finally come around.

'Could Tytti and I have a moment alone,' said Anna, dismissing Teemu. Opening his mouth to protest but then thinking better of it, Teemu stepped out of the office.

'It's bad for business,' hissed Anna, in case Teemu were listening outside the door. 'I'm trying to start up a hotel. You should have had the sense to not write a word!'

'How can you fire me! I was only doing my job,' whispered Tytti angrily.

'Well, you should know better. You have no discretion, Tytti. Constable Mansikka-aho hasn't even come back to you with the results of Dr Wahlroos's tests! Yes, I phoned and checked. I was doing your job, I suppose!' whispered back Anna harshly. They were both red-faced and angry.

'You cannot be trusted, Tytti. Trust is everything to me. Life is about favours done and who owes whom. Can't you see that you stupid girl!'

Tytti recoiled in shock. Now Anna was going too far.

'And you are wrong!' said Tytti, her voice rising. 'Life is about honesty and openness. I'm not going to lie about an event by omission!'

Anna paused and stood ominously still. Then, as if the altercation had never taken place, she began, 'There is one thing you can do to make sure it's only a suspension. Sit down.'

Sitting in the chair, Tytti felt uneasy whenever Anna drifted out of view or wandered behind her.

'Stay out of it, Tytti. Whoever put that skull in the tree wants trouble. But I have it under control. Stay out of it and you can return to work.'

Chapter Eighteen

Tytti returned home to the same cold house she had departed from that morning and dumped down her backpack. Stacking some logs inside the stove that provided her heat, she struck a match and, using some old candle ends as firelighters, lit the newspaper. Some might consider burning your own newspaper a crime, but on that day Tytti felt it to be purifying.

As the house was so cold, Tytti sat out on her porch with her laptop on her knees. Aged nets and dormant wire fishing baskets hung swaying from the beams. Interesting old shells and bits of gnarled wood lay on the window-ledge. Things she had collected as an old seadog.

Her internet searches of the Names, Births and Deaths Register had been a success. Anna had been born in 1961, the same year as Heike Tapio, her first husband, making them both only sixteen when they married. Cross-referencing with newspaper cuttings, Tytti managed to find a picture of their nuptials in 1977. It had been a traditional castle wedding, with rather untraditional dress. Anna had worn a white maxi-dress and floppy hat, while her bridesmaids had been draped in canary yellow with a startling geometric design.

A typical *à la mode* seventies wedding, thought Tytti. Then she read that Heike Tapio had drowned just before Terhi had been born and Anna had become a widow. So early on, thought Tytti, comparing the dates. They only had eight months together. Think of the sorrow Anna must have felt. Then Karl Tapio, her father-in-law and the castle owner, died. 'Cause unknown,' said the Deaths Register.

Anna had married the poet Simo Salama, in 1991. Tytti also found a picture of these later nuptials. The article said that the picture was of a secret wedding that had taken place in a registry office in order to avoid press intrusion. It was a far more informal affair than the first, with Anna in a short white dress and no sword at Simo's side. From another article she gleaned that Anna had married Simo at the height of his career. Tytti knew several of his poems. One of them had supposedly been written about Anna, but Tytti could not remember which one.

Still feeling resentful and bullied, Tytti decided to intensify her investigation rather than let it go. She would just have to use some of that discretion Anna cherished so much. Now she wondered whether there might be a feature budding beneath all the research she was doing. Maybe Juha at *Helsingin Sanomat* would print it under the title: 'The Truth about Anna Tapio'?

That would be a way to retaliate, thought Tytti.

As the evening drew on, strained by her recent traumas and all the revengeful research, she snapped shut her laptop, yawned, and went inside to lie down on her bed. How had it come to this? She had been let go. Her world was turning upside down.

Dozing off, she only awoke when the wind suddenly blew her door open. Still tired, she got up and closed it, extinguished the fire, and decided an early night was in order. Switching off the light, she undressed and went to lie down. Her bed was an old-style Finnish bed with a high wooden back along one of the long sides, and two high ends. It was a bit like sleeping in a three-sided box. It had been there long before Tytti had, and she had chosen not to change it.

She awoke to the ricochet of her own choking. The room was filled with the acrid tang of smoke. The embers of the fire had still been alight when Tytti went to bed, but the damper had been closed and the stove door firmly shut. No air could have got to the cinders, and they would have extinguished on their own. But now the room was filled with smoke.

Suffocating in the bitter whiteness, Tytti managed to get to the stove and close the hot oven door on the newly catching fire. Coughing and spluttering, she ran outside, leaving the door open to try and disperse the smoke.

Outside, she began to regain her senses.

Why on earth was the oven door open? she wondered. I definitely closed it before I went to sleep.

Tytti also noted that she had forgotten to lock the door. Something she had done many times before but which was now a fact that seemed pertinent. Could somebody have relit the fire and left the oven door open to asphyxiate her in her sleep? Standing on the porch, she began to realise just how lucky she had been to wake up in the nick of time. She started to shake from the shock; the chilled midnight air added to her trembling.

She heard a stick snap in the forest behind the house, and froze. She felt exposed and vulnerable. But she could not go back into the house yet, it was still full of smoke. There was nowhere to find sanctuary. Had that been the idea? To run her out of the house? Or was she being paranoid?

She glanced around for a weapon. If somebody was going to jump her, then she was going to give them hell. Having never hit, well, anything, she was not sure how this hell would be arrived at; but knowing it to be a matter of survival, she hoped her animal instincts would kick in and do the business.

Picking up a broom, she felt fear as well as anger, but anger began to gain the upper hand and she took a silent breath. Following the path round to the back of the house, she paused at the corner. She had a feeling she was being watched. There was a movement behind a tree. As her eyes adjusted to the dark, she peered into the undergrowth and heard a rustle. Her heart stopped as she saw two eyes staring back at her. Then she saw a black and white face. Her heart began to slow as a badger turned and fled, startled by the naked lady with the broom.

Tytti exhaled. It must have been an accident. She must not have closed the stove door properly. It was her own fault then. Walking back round to the porch, she looked out to sea and thought she saw a flash. A glint of light in the bay, where the waters were too shallow for the larger boats.

It must be a small boat, she thought. She scanned the sea again, but did not see the light. Maybe she had imagined it. But a spectre of doubt crept over her, and she began to wonder if the smoky room had been an accident after all.

Chapter Nineteen

'Problem.' Tytti plumped herself down into one of the squashy chairs in Ritva's bookshop. Taking the statement as a question, Ritva thought for a moment and then replied.

'Not a problem yet. But see that man who's just left? He's from the council. He came in to inspect the premises. Why they want to inspect a bookshop I can't understand. But then they suggested that my bookshop is actually a coffee shop and so in violation of a number of codes.'

Tytti stopped angrily glancing through that day's *Helsingin Sanomat* and gave Ritva her full attention.

'It seems I require a licence stating that the bookshop is actually a coffee shop or else end the coffee part of my enterprise.' Ritva sighed. 'The most distressing thing is that if I take out this licence, then Lili won't be allowed in anymore — and Lili and I are inseparable.'

'What do you intend to do?'

'Well, carry on as normal I suppose. These things take time and there's no way I could leave Lili at home. She'd pine for me.' They both looked down at a sleeping Lili, tucked up in a ball. Who would dare to upset such an arrangement? 'Anyway, that's enough about that. Let's talk about my date with Kai. That'll take my mind off things.' Ritva continued, 'We were given a nice cosy corner table so I was sitting quite close to him. It made me a bit nervous but I don't think he really noticed. For some reason I couldn't relax properly. I think it might have had something to do with, despite the best intentions, being rather bored.'

'You found him boring?' Tytti asked in surprise.

'Yes, don't you? I didn't really know how to handle the end of the meal. If he asked for another date, I thought I'd say no. But then I thought, I must be mad! Here was a handsome man sitting next to me. Wouldn't it be crazy not to go on another date with him just because I wasn't attracted to him? And then I started to worry about what you'd say if I turned down another date. If he didn't ask, well, what a relief; but otherwise I would have to say yes. That was when he asked me so of course I said yes. But then it seemed my fortunes changed. He had to rush off — but he left a fifty-euro tip!'

'That's substantial.'

'That's excessive. I swapped it for zero and left. He's rich, Tytti, and, more importantly, generous! He would make someone, possibly me, a fine husband — a trophy husband. It doesn't really matter that I don't find him interesting, funny or even sexually attractive. Plenty of women marry men for reasons other than those. I'll just have to put up with it. And then I began to think that we must be a good match, else you would not have set us up in the first place.'

Ritva smiled widely at Tytti. She had begun to feel much brighter about her future and her expenditure in it. She drew in a deep breath. Tytti remained silent, beginning to feel dread. 'I think I'm going to marry him. I like him — I just don't really like him in that way. But he likes me, and I got to thinking what a good catch he is. I mean, he's good-looking, rich, he lives in a castle. I'd be mad to let him get away.'

Tytti stayed silent. She would have preferred to be talking about the threat to Lili's happiness. Then, on this rarest of occasions, she raised the subject she most feared.

'But what about love, Ritva? Do you think you could fall in love with him? Surely you'd want to be with a man that you loved?'

'I've tried that. You've said yourself that I make terrible choices when it comes to men, and here's a lovely man that wants to go on another date!'

Tytti sighed. The one time Ritva had really listened to her opinion was now going to be used as an excuse to start a relationship with Kai. It was all wrong. Ritva was desperate to get married, that was the problem. She did not seem to care much about who it would be, she just wanted to tie the knot again. And Tytti had helped her to get Kai. Tytti felt annoyed with herself. But Ritva was her friend. What could she do?

'Don't do it, Ritva. It's not the right thing to do. You mustn't trick him into providing for you by pretending you're in love with him. You mustn't use love like that, as an act, as a lure. It's a terrible thing to do.'

'What do you mean, "terrible"? Don't you want me to be happy? I could be happy with Kai. Look at all the things I'd have. I'd be married to a wealthy and influential man who could look after me. None of those other losers ever looked after me, they always looked after number one first and last. Well I've learnt my lesson! I'm going to do what they did to me. They used me when I was completely smitten with them. I'm not going to be a doormat anymore, I'm going to be in the driving seat, and the only way to do that is to be with somebody I do not love!'

'But it's the wrong thing to do,' continued Tytti. 'You cannot do this. It's wrong.'

But Ritva had stopped listening.

Tytti sat there in annoyance. She hated having this confrontation with Ritva, and found that her fists were clenched. It was not a serious fight, and the bond between them was strong enough for her to not feel insecure about their friendship, but she did feel awful. And it had been her own fault for setting up two friends on a date. Now Kai was to be made to suffer by Ritva's rotten behaviour. How could she be so cold! Years of being hurt, she supposed; but that was no real excuse.

Tytti wondered whether she should share with Ritva the recent events — and someone's attempt to silence her. The way Ritva was looking at her, she was not sure she would keep this quiet. Particularly from Kai. No, Ritva was not one to keep a secret. She had talked about Tytti to others in the past without Tytti's knowledge. Tytti had only found out about it when Ritva herself had told her! Ritva could not be trusted to keep any secret, even her own, and especially not one as important as this.

Chapter Twenty

Sawdust from the woodcutter's carvings sprinkled on the grass. Smoke from the smithy lingering in the air. The midnight sun, and the white night. All these things brought back memories for Tytti. Growing up, she had never missed the Midsummer's celebration on the island. A place where respected traditions were re-enacted in a time-honoured manner.

As the local theatre group wrapped up their play about the history of Finland, the lottery-picked winners, a girl from Helsinki and a boy from Barcelona, who had married that afternoon at the island's church, arrived in procession to dance the first dance on stage. Then, as custom dictated, they rode down to the shore in a small cart to meet the church boat, a long boat that carried them to an outcrop of rock on the sea where an unlit bonfire stood, a conical pile of dry brush, made perfectly ready by the preceding warm nights.

A crackling announcement told the people to move down to the shore. The murmuring crowd did so. Now everybody was waiting for the church boat to arrive. It came, paddled off, and then the groom stood ready to ignite the bonfire. He poked nervously with a lighted torch until the wood caught and leapt with flame.

Through an oil-like shimmer of heat, Tytti looked out at the spectators in their boats crisscrossing the sea. Her feet ached from gripping the rough granite of a boulder that offered the perfect vantage point to view the bonfire. She had been standing for over an hour now, but this was the pinnacle of the Midsummer's celebrations, and a welcome reprieve from the recent disaster that was Tytti's life. Surrounded by laughter and song, she let herself go, joining in the festive cheer, her position next to the band lending itself to joyful behaviour. Dressed like dolls, women in national costume stood dotted around the crowd, their hair in long pigtails, below-the-knee red skirts with coloured and patterned ribbon trimmings, blue waistcoats and baggy white shirts. A woman and her daughter, each with a crown of flowers on her head, held hands and sang along to the first verse of the traditional summer hymn *Suvivirsi*.

> *'The precious season has come and summer sweet. Every place is beautifully blossoming with flowers. Now the warmth of the sun brings blessings, nature is restored, inviting life.'*

'Long live Finland,' thought Tytti, enveloped by the atmosphere. Yes, Finland! At twenty-five she thought she understood what the world was, and if you could find a little piece to live quietly on then you were inordinately lucky. Here in Finland there were such places, and Tytti was one of the fortunate ones. Yes, the world was turning upside down. China was holding a Gay Pride event while America was refuting gay marriage. Cricket fixtures were being moved from India to South Africa because of security concerns. Yes, the world was slowly changing.

Then she saw Denis standing on the ground at the bottom of the boulder.

'Denis!' she shouted, but he could not hear her above the music.

As the festivities came to an end, a breathless Tytti carefully climbed down the rock and caught Denis by the shoulder. They looked at each other, each of them smiling, and shared a moment of Finnish magic.

'Tytti! I'm glad to see you. I've been looking out for you all evening.' They walked among the milling throng.

'This morning I went back up to the castle stables to go back to the spot where the silver bar was found. But on my way—I was nearly there—I saw somebody go into the woods! I couldn't see who it was, I was still some distance off. And I don't know why, but something about them made me stop and not want to follow them in.'

'Maybe it was a berry-picker.'

'That was my first thought as well. But it does seem kind of an odd place to be picking berries. So out-of-the-way of any other forest, and next to the sea. I didn't notice any berries when we were up there anyhow. No, I think somebody is onto us. Somebody knows there might be a silver hoard up there.'

But who? thought Tytti. The only people she was aware of who knew about the silver bar were the Tapio family and Ulrich. Kai and Ulrich had already searched up there, and the others had not seemed the remotest bit interested in it. For a moment, Tytti felt annoyance at Denis for not following whoever it was into the forest and simply asking them what they were doing there. But then, Denis was very insecure, and her reprimand would only make him feel bad.

'I suppose I should really have gone after them,' Denis said now, seeing her look of annoyance. That sinking feeling he got so often when he thought he had disappointed someone began to wash over him. He bowed his head and nervously stopped making eye contact with Tytti.

'Well, never mind,' said Tytti, seeing Denis's hangdog expression. 'We'll just have to keep an eye out in case they return.'

They had reached the other side of the wooden footbridge that joined the path back to civilisation. Tytti went to try and extract her bicycle from the tangle of others. Denis put on his moped helmet and got ready to head off. Then he said the words that Tytti had been waiting for but had been dreading to hear.

'Er, maybe, if you came up there the next time, if the person is up there, well, two heads are better than one,' said Denis meekly.

His lack of confidence was the stick to beat Tytti into agreeing to go up there with him again.

If only there was a carrot, thought Tytti. If only.

Chapter Twenty-one

Cycling to work after her suspension, Tytti was looking forward to her day. The sun shone, the dew glowed, the air around her was silent and peaceful. Arriving at the market square, she dismounted from her bicycle and pushed it over the cobblestones towards the bookshop.

Tytti gently opened the bookshop door. Unfazed by her recent suspension, she had used the time to continue her investigations. And she planned to start today with a lie — or a half-truth, anyway.

Lili ambled over to say hello. Ritva was quietly standing next to a dustbin with a strange look on her face, a look Tytti had never seen before. Her eyebrows were raised as if in surprise above lips pursed in contemplation. She was holding a letter taken from a large brown envelope.

'So, er, how are you today?' asked Tytti, unsure of the answer she would receive.

'Not bad,' said Ritva, surprising Tytti.

Ritva looked at Tytti and smiled, her odd mood vanishing at the sight of her good friend. Ritva was resilient, and even during troubled times was known to be a happy individual. A good person to arrange a funeral, perhaps.

'And how are you today?' she asked.

'Very good,' said Tytti, slightly surprising herself. 'What are you holding?'

Ritva passed the letter to Tytti. She was immediately drawn to the livid red typeface: 'Book shop considered to be a coffee shop and will be closed in four weeks if conditions not met and permit unapproved.'

There was no stamp on the letter. The man from the council had swooped in the night. Tytti passed the letter back.

'Well, Mr —,' said Ritva reading the name . aloud, 'what are you afraid of, hairs in the coffee? Well, this is what I think of you, Mr —,' and Ritva tossed the notice into the bin.

After the ritual of coffee being poured and pleasantries exchanged, Tytti decided to broach her theme. As Ritva sat down, Tytti enquired, 'Can I borrow Lili? You see, I'm writing an article on the dog park and I need to go and visit it.'

Ritva tensed. The solitary gurgle of the coffee machine could be heard.

'You don't need a dog to go to the dog park. Dogless people are allowed in as well.' Ritva was extremely protective of Lili and the thought of anything happening to her when she was not there troubled her. What if another dog bit her? A larger dog with nasty breath. Ritva tensed even more. 'So, what precisely will the story be about?'

Tytti had primed herself for resistance and

prepared well.

'It's an article on dog parks, their benefits and liabilities. To write a word I need to enter the world of dogs in a clandestine way. The wrong people will always talk to you if they know you're a journalist. I'd like to be able to hear the quieter voice that would clam up under those circumstances.' She felt she had put her point across rather succinctly.

'So, you'll be spying on dog owners? Are you sure that's ethical?'

Tytti pondered, thinking about her illicit view from behind the slatted blind.

'Well, I don't know. Nobody ever asks, do they? Nobody ever really says, "Excuse me, I'll be covertly watching you today. Possibly with a pair of binoculars. Does anybody mind?"'

Gazing at their knees, Lili, still sleepy, lay on her side, up on an armchair. She had heard her name mentioned and was now waiting for the word 'meatball' or 'treat' to be intoned before she bothered to move her head. Nothing forthcoming, she decided that she had better check on her biscuits, which she had strategically placed around the bookshop. Locals had learnt to avoid them, and it was only the odd tourist who jumped as they crunched one flat. Lili did not like this. Lili did not like tourists who stood on her biscuits. Seeing one coming, she would quickly run to it and pick it up in her mouth. Sometimes she would pick up as many as three at a time — a masterful feat for such a small dog.

'Well, okay then. Seeing as it's important for the well-being of dogs. You can take her this evening.'

Chapter Twenty-two

Kai returned despondently to his neatly arranged desk. He had just come from an unsuccessful meeting with the local bank. Their advertising revenue had been the same for a long time, and the bank was refusing to lend any more money to prop up production costs. Cash flow was severely restricted and bills had begun to go unpaid. It looked like they might be going out of business fairly soon.

Apart from the repeat advertising, the latest advert to be placed had been over a fortnight ago and, curiously, had been for a magician looking for an assistant.

Wanted: a narrow woman with a very long torso, the advert had read. *Flexibility an advantage*. The man was obviously an amateur.

Tytti strolled over to the newspaper office and propped up her bicycle outside. She could just make out Kai sitting aimlessly at his desk. He was lost in thought, shifting bits of paper around, shaking his mouse to get rid of the screen saver, occasionally tapping the keyboard of his computer. Now he had stopped to poke a pot plant.

'Bored?' suggested Tytti as she entered the

office.

'Just a bit.' Teemu was away on holiday, and Kai's mother, Anna, had ordered him to 'look after things' in his absence.

'Sometimes it's fun to have a whisky and smoke and just sit back and read old editions. That qualifies as work in Teemu's mind.' She had often smelt cigar smoke coming from under the closed door and the whisky fumes on Teemu's breath when he had come outside to bother her. Tytti had been enjoying the peace of having Teemu away. 'It's usually quite useful, to stimulate new ideas and follow-ups.'

'Well, I don't smoke, so that one's out, and the whisky sounds good in theory, but I think I'd better wait until after work to explore that option.'

As it should be, thought Tytti. Kai was turning out to be a far better boss than Teemu. Or did she just think that because years of Teemu had taken their toll?

It is never healthy to see so much of a person in such a confined space for such a long time, she thought, and for a split second she had some rather dark thoughts about Teemu never returning—due to some tragic accident. She remembered the first day Teemu had arrived. Busying himself around the place but accomplishing nothing. Once, in his office, Tytti had noticed that he wrote out a weekly list of things to do and gradually crossed them off, one by one. Often, that short list would last a week.

'Do you think we could maybe get people to pay to be interviewed?' asked Kai.

'Bad practice, I'm afraid. Although I know of a few local councillors and business people who might be interested in a favourable feature on their supposedly "overlooked" efforts. Maybe we could slant some articles to be of benefit to them in some way. And add a line at the end with their contact details. That's usually what they're after when they ring me at the office— they either have something to sell or some event to promote.'

'If only they would just cough up and advertise,' said Kai. 'The paper could really do with the money.'

Tytti balked.

'Is the newspaper in that much trouble?'

'No, we won't have to fold,' said Kai uncertainly, 'But the paper's coverage of the news is somewhat sketchy, and our features can't compete with those of the bigger newspapers.'

'Is it too late to save it?' asked Tytti, shocked. She had had the utmost confidence in Kai's ability to fix the paper's financial problems.

Kai did not answer. Deep in thought about these problems, he decided to keep them to himself.

'It's never too late.'

Rather than whisky, the smell of chips now wafted through the office, reminding them both that the new recycling lorry, which ran on cooking oil, was on its way round. It was Recycling Day.

Kai went to collect the paper bin, pausing to check his organised desk for anything unwanted. Tytti chased an empty paper coffee cup that had rolled under her desk.

Kai studied Tytti's workspace. He wondered whether it might be time to broach the topic of a clear-desk policy. He had noticed that there were boxes and folders for various things jumbled around her desk — a desk covered in paper and multicoloured sticky notes. Could Tytti really be working on so many projects? It seemed unlikely. It appeared that anything was allowed to set up camp there. But maybe Tytti was one of those people who knew exactly where things were among the chaos?

Kai spotted a folded piece of paper shoved under one leg of Tytti's desk. Not wanting to annoy her, he waited for her to go into the kitchen, then pulled out the piece of paper. He unfolded it to see if it was important, and read the first line. As he read on, he started to realise that the sheet contained notes on his family.

The sound of a cupboard closing in the kitchen reminded him that Tytti was on her way back, and he stuffed the piece of paper back under the desk leg. What could this mean? Suddenly Kai felt a moment of doubt. Had he been wrong to trust Tytti and bring her into the inner circle of his family? She was, after all, a journalist. Then he cringed at his own snobbish thoughts. *Not noble and just a journalist.*

Chapter Twenty-three

The little dog park was only recognisable among the weeds by a faded black bench in the shape of a sausage dog. Just in case, Tytti pulled a waste bag from the dispenser by the gate. Lili had relieved herself on the walk there but Tytti knew that there might be an elusive second poo. As she opened the gate, the grating of the metal brought the other little dogs over, alerted that a newcomer had arrived. Tytti closed the metal gate to prevent the little mutts from escaping and released Lili from her lead. Free at last, she sprinted a circuit of the park and then began her favourite game of taunting the other dogs by sitting down whenever one tried to sniff her behind.

Tytti sat down on the dog-shaped bench, which was covered in muddy paw marks and, she hoped, droplets from a recent shower. There were at that moment four other little dogs in the park, the owners standing chatting to each other in a comfortable way about their dogs and their habits. Although they had nodded "hello" when she had entered, Tytti did not feel it would be right to cut in, and so she waited in silence.

The dog park emptied and became still. Maybe Tytti had missed her chance by not talking to the other owners? Then the metal guard on the gate clanked noisily once more. A woman with a large dog had decided to come in. Tytti jumped up, ready to gather up Lili so she would not be knocked over or sat upon by this substantially larger dog. She called out, but Lili was too busy watching the new arrival to bother even to pretend to hear. Not willing to take a chance, Tytti dashed over and scooped her up.

'Your dog is big!' shouted Tytti across the park.

The lady glanced at her and replied, 'Yes, but she is gentle.'

Tytti decided to sit down and hold Lili on her knees in order to meet this unwelcome dog which, in fact, had begun to sniff Lili's face in a more friendly than hungry way. Taking matters into her own paws, Lili bounded from Tytti's knees and raced away for a game of chase with the newcomer. At this point, the lady came over. She was around fifty and wore a hand-knitted jumper of fuzzy blue and red, a long tweed skirt, washed-out grey woollen tights, and orange fingerless gloves. She wore a magenta felt hat with a mass of faded green undergrowth poked under the band.

'What kind of dog is that?' asked Tytti, relieved that conflict had been avoided.

'Mongrel. Don't know what kind. Parents must have been mongrels too. Maybe even her grandparents. She is gentle with little dogs but doesn't like big ones. Or people—big or little.

Maybe she gets that from me.'

'Do you think she has any German Shepherd in her?'

'Possibly. A man stood over there in the bush one day. He shouted at me. Called me names and threw a beer can at me. Just a drunk, I guess; but he scared me. Ella went berserk protecting me. Ran up and down the fence she did, trying to get at the man. Now I feel safe. Even when I walk her in the dark in the woods.' In Finland half the year was dark and much time was spent by dog owners tramping with torches through parks and forests.

'Yes, German Shepherds are renowned for their loyalty and bravery, aren't they? That's why the police and army use them. In fact, I'm thinking about getting one. Do you know anybody around here that has one?'

The woman gazed up at the treetops as she considered Tytti's question.

'Not many birds this year,' she said. Tytti waited for her answer.

'See, there was once a man who threatened me. Ella protected me. She is a very good dog. I feel safe with her now.'

Once the confused lady had left, the dog park remained quiet. Tytti sat down again and looked in the direction where the little dog fence met the big dog fence. After hours of patient waiting, Lili was sick of it and wanted to go home for her supper. Her little paws had grown cold and she now sat next to Tytti on the bench. Tytti had decided that this might be the only chance she would get to borrow Lili, and so was hanging on in the hope that somebody, anybody, might appear with a German Shepherd.

The gate to the big dog park clanged open and a man wearing a red baseball cap entered. He held a large tan and black dog on a leash. The dog held an apple-green tennis ball in its mouth.

Tytti decided it was time to do some bird-watching, and uncased her binoculars.

Pretending to peer up at the sky to observe the birds (of which there were none), Tytti diverted her gaze towards the man. He was tall, and a tuft of dark-brown hair stuck out from the back of his cap. Could this be the author of the letter?

Thirty minutes later, it was time to act. The man and his dog were leaving the park. But Lili had other ideas. She wanted to go home and, when Tytti pointed her in the opposite direction to home, she simply sat down and glued herself to the floor. Tytti pulled on the lead. Nothing happened. Man and dog were getting away.

Not wanting to miss her opportunity, Tytti squatted down and tried to reason with Lili. When Lili refused to be coerced, Tytti sighed, leaned over, and picked her up. With a despondent Lili in her arms, Tytti followed the man, who was now fairly far ahead.

After ten minutes or so, and with shoulders aching, she had followed him to the top of a dead-end road.

Should I go after him some more? Tytti wondered, trying to loosen up her sore arms and shoulders. But then she might draw attention to herself, carrying a dog that refused to walk. Then she remembered that he knew what she looked like. Whoever had planted the letter had certainly recognised her cardigan on the evening of the hotel opening.

Deciding against it, she set Lili down on the ground and, to Lili's relief, turned to take her home.

Chapter Twenty-four

'Oh, Tytti, the meal was a disaster. Anna clearly hated me, and Ulrich just sat there in silence. The only time he spoke was to say what he did for a living. He's an investment banker and venture capitalist, whatever that means. He seemed rather puffed up about it,' Ritva told Tytti as she returned Lili. She had just endured the unfortunate experience of dining with Kai, Anna and Ulrich.

'She asked me if I had any noble blood in me! What a question! Who would ask such a thing in Finland!'

Tytti remembered several articles that she had read about Anna in the papers. She had once been a glamorous it-girl, often spotted about town in Helsinki. She was probably after a carbon copy of herself for Kai: a tall, slim girl with platinum-blonde hair. Ideally, an aristocrat with her family record held at the House of Nobility to verify it. Imposters were not welcome.

So, they didn't get on, thought Tytti, giving Ritva a sympathetic smile.

Showing a moment of clarity, Ritva continued, 'Anna seems sad and cruel at the same time. She was angry about Terhi's situation and furious with Kai about something. She openly despised me and called me a "shop girl". I had to explain to her that I was the proprietress of a bookshop. I think she classes me as some kind of librarian, a career I did actually look into once. And anyway, what is so wrong with being a librarian?' said Ritva forcefully.

Tytti smiled in agreement, letting Ritva continue her rant.

'It was strange to see myself through her eyes. I felt like a loser. And then, later on, Kai and Ulrich got food poisoning. They'd ordered the same fish dish. Pike perch with carrot risotto, fennel and herb mayonnaise—would you believe. At the time they both said that it tasted marvellous despite not thinking they would like the fennel. But a few hours later they were throwing up.

Tytti smiled secretly to herself at the image of Ulrich vomiting. But then she thought of Kai and felt a ripple of sympathy.

Ritva could contain herself no longer.

'Why are you smirking at me! I'm repeating this awful affair to you and you're sneering at me?'

Tytti was dumbfounded.

'I bet you're annoyed with me because I got to spend time with Anna and Ulrich, aren't you? You think they're your domain. I bet you're glad that they thought so little of me!'

Tytti's jaw dropped.

'Well, I've got Kai, not you!'

That was quick, thought Tytti. But then, this was Ritva — so perhaps it was a reasonable time frame after all.

The problem was that there was an element of truth in what Ritva said. Just one grain. A grain that, when focussed on, made the wider picture seem true. But only a slower, deeper analysis could really show the whole matter: that Tytti liked Kai — as a friend. They had known each other for years and she felt affection for him. Ritva was a quick, if random, arbitrator.

'But I'm not jealous of you and Kai! I'm glad that you've finally met somebody so easily,' Tytti protested. That had not come out right.

'So, do you think I'm the one who's jealous? And you think I'm doing this because it's convenient, do you? Well, for your information, we haven't slept together yet.'

Somehow this made Tytti feel a little better. She did not desire Kai, not in the least, but it seemed that Ritva had got it into her head that she did. In truth it was Ritva who felt insecure about her relationship with Kai and the Tapios, and she had extended her claws to keep others away — including her attractive best friend.

Tytti began to feel angry at being accused of enjoying Ritva's discomfort. But then was Ritva not in it for the money? For the status of being Mrs Kai Tapio? Tytti would not endorse that, and pushed away all thoughts of sympathy. Maybe this disastrous dinner would be enough to make Ritva see the madness of her plan.

Angry at Ritva's suggestions, Tytti bicycled
furiously over to Tapiolinna. Finland—her
beautiful Finland, one of the most egalitarian
countries in the world when it came to the
sexes—was about to be let down by Ritva, a
woman with ulterior motives. Tytti thought
back to something she had read in her father's
notes. To a sad but common story. There were
still women who became 'accidentally' pregnant
and expected the man to provide. Inevitably,
these couples broke up, often after domestic
violence had taken its toll. A man beats his wife
to try and make her leave him. The wife feigns
love and is willing to do anything to make him
stay. A man stuck with a cold woman and a
child he never wanted. Trapped, unable to take
the child, and expected to pay for the woman.
These men always cheated and went on to the
next woman. History would then repeat itself.
　　'No!' thought Tytti, leaning forward,
gripping the handlebars and cycling even faster.
No, Tytti could not let Kai become that man!
She had to tell him the truth!

Chapter Twenty-five

'Kai's not here,' said Terhi. 'But he shouldn't be long coming back. Why not join me for a drink?'

It was still light, so they sat outside on the terrace. Terhi suggested a glass of wine and Tytti agreed, welcoming any biochemical change that would ease her fury. She was not about to spoil her time with Terhi just because Ritva was being an idiot.

She looks exhausted, thought Tytti as she sat down on the patio chair.

It was true: investment banking had been no preparation for motherhood. Terhi had lost touch with her friends, as she had never had time for them. But then, in the dog-eat-dog world of banking, not having friends was not unusual. But now she felt very alone and unsure of herself. And back at the home she grew up in, painful memories of being rejected by her mother had begun to rear their own ugly heads. A needy Terhi remembered the arguments she had had with Anna, particularly the one when her mother had screamed at her, 'I fed you, didn't I!' in response to Terhi's question as to why her mother did not seem to like her. To Anna, Terhi had an infuriating need to get closer to her — a need that Anna rejected. That argument had come about when Terhi had been a teenager. Anna could not handle having another person question her, especially a challenging thirteen-year-old. So she did to Terhi what she did to everybody else: she treated her with contempt. But Terhi still loved her, and was desperate for that love to be returned. Even as a troubled adult, she still ran back to her, foolishly hoping that she would find a safe place to rest. In her fantasy, her mother loved her and welcomed her home. But once more she had been crushed, and then angry with herself for believing her own fantasy.

'I hear that Kai has been seeing your friend Ritva,' said Terhi as she sipped her water.

Tytti stayed silent.

'That's just what I heard.'

'Hmm,' said Tytti, noncommittal.

'He seems to be quite keen on her.'

Tytti wondered whether or not she should keep Ritva's secret. Ritva had put her in an awkward position. Tytti's take on life involved being honest. Straightforward and truthful. But could she do this to her best friend? Would Ritva ever allow her to forget it? Was Tytti really upright enough to tell Terhi the truth? Give Kai a heads-up so he had a chance to get away?

Those unfair accusations from Ritva still jabbered in her mind as she spoke. Had it been another time — if Tytti had not felt so resentful and had had time to cool off — then the answer to the question might have been quite different.

'She wants him for his money.'

'Er, what…?'

'His money. She wants him for it.'

Unsure she had heard correctly, Terhi prompted her.

'Did you say Ritva only wants Kai for his money?'

'His money and his status. She doesn't like him at all.' Tytti thought she would feel better after this declaration, feel a weight lift from her shoulders; but she felt no release, only a mess of emotions.

Eyebrows raised, Terhi caught her breath in wonder at the news. She would have to be the bearer of this intelligence to her brother, something she did not relish. She knew how much he wanted to get married and settle down. She also knew how paranoid he was about being used for his wealth and position.

'Anyway, that's that,' stated Tytti, mentally dusting her hands of all responsibility. 'How are things with you?'

This was the question Terhi had been waiting desperately for someone to ask her. And now it had come, she could not hold back. She took a sip of her water. Her face remained impassive, but tears began to run down her cheeks.

'I…' said Terhi, dabbing her tears with the tissue that was clasped in her hand. She wanted to say more. She needed to say more.

Assertive, outspoken and driven to lead, Terhi could, according to her CV, 'understand difficult organisational problems and create solid solutions.' But in this case, she was unable to get anywhere close. Although intelligent and well-informed, Terhi, who valued competence and had little patience for inefficiency, had created a disaster. She felt lost, hopeless, disconnected from her situation.

'I… I think I've messed things up. I was working long hours. In a stressful job. I didn't eat the right food. I didn't sleep enough, go to yoga, or do any of the things I was supposed to do. I'm sick all the time. And I just can't sleep. It's all my fault, and John, my old boss and the baby's father, wants nothing to do with me. He says he is a happily married man and the fling was a mistake. A mistake that he actively pursued for several months.'

Tytti saw the tears stop falling and Terhi's cheeks flush pink with fury.

Tytti paused and wondered how to console her.

'It must be difficult to be you,' said Tytti. 'So critical of yourself.'

Terhi sniffed and gave a bizarre laugh. Tytti had heard of such things. A first trimester could be fraught with depression. And Terhi had been bottling it all up. She was allowed to be sad and hate how she felt. Especially as nausea was keeping her isolated at the castle.

'I feel trapped inside this body, inside my

mind. I need to escape.' The tears had dried and she just looked defeated now. Tytti thought long and hard about what she was about to say.

'We are never the prisoners of our fate,' said Tytti, 'and it must be horrible to be trapped inside your own head. To be suffering inside your mind and to feel you have no escape.'

Terhi looked sharply up. And Tytti knew that she was right.

'I was just so tired that I lost track of what I'd already taken. The doctor just told me to be more careful in the future. I don't know if I was really trying to overdose.'

They both sat quietly for a while absorbing the words.

'What kind of pills were they?'

'Sleeping. I guess it's common to blame the parents for not being emotionally involved when a situation like this happens. I think I'm a bit old to pass blame, though.'

'Your father is dead, right?'

'Yes, he died before I was born. I don't feel like I've missed out on anything, though. I had nothing to miss, if you know what I mean.'

'Yes,' said Tytti, 'I lost my mother when I was very young. I couldn't remember her, so I didn't miss her. I guess we both understood the situation, and happiness came from that understanding. Maybe as you come to understand your situation, you will begin to be happy again too. A person can have a horrible life and still be happy, if they are aware of

what's what. You can feel safe in knowing that
to be true.'

Chapter Twenty-six

The next morning, peering into driveways and looking for clues, Tytti wandered to the bottom of the dead-end lane along which she had followed the man with the German Shepherd. A dilapidated seventies house lay on her left and a pale-yellow and white traditional house stood opposite. Strolling towards the seventies house, Tytti stopped and looked over the chain-link padlocked gate. The neighbour in the traditional home was gardening, on her knees eliminating weeds from about her geraniums. Tytti moved closer and waited for the woman to notice her.

'Beautiful day, isn't it?' smiled Tytti when the neighbour looked up.

'Yes,' said the neighbour, straightening up and catching her hair in a crab apple tree.

'I wonder,' said Tytti, 'does a dark-haired man live in the house opposite?'

The woman gave her a long look.

'Why do you ask?' She looked suspicious. But then Tytti could have been a dreaded tax inspector, a debt collector, an ex-wife… Not just an honest journalist. Tytti decided to try another tack.

'Does he own a German Shepherd dog?'

'No,' said the woman, and Tytti believed

her. Apologising for disturbing her, she turned away. Walking off, she could feel the eyes of the gardening neighbour follow her. Possibly taking a mental picture in case of a future incident.

At the end of the road was the beginning of a footpath. Ducking under a bush, Tytti began to follow a narrow, haphazard track. A short cut — but to where? At the end of the track, she had to use a root to help her slide down a rock face that landed at the island's harbour. It was not a very large harbour but it did have a diesel station for the boats. An attendant was sitting there in an old white wire chair reading one of the Finnish red-tops. Tytti noticed, with a twinge of guilt, that her story about the skull had been featured on the cover of the tabloid. Word had spread.

'Excuse me,' she asked, 'have any boats docked here recently with a dog on board?' Barely looking up, the attendant pointed out two boats.

'Estonian and Russian.'

Tytti thanked him and began to walk down to the jetty to explore further. Instinct told her to go to the boat farthest away, an old rusty white fishing boat. A tattered tricolour flag with three equal horizontal bands of blue, black and white hung lifelessly on a diagonal pole. The Estonian flag. Peering over the side, Tytti saw a large water-bowl on the deck. Suspecting that any dog on board would have been barking at her long before her arrival, Tytti surmised that nobody was around. Now was her chance to investigate and see whether this man was the author of the letter.

Climbing onto the deck across the watery gap between boat and dock, Tytti could see that the boat had a hatch that led to a cabin in the hull. She pulled open the heavy hatch door. Climbing down the almost vertical wooden steps, her heart began to beat faster. If he returned now, especially with the dog, she would not be in a good position. Then she noticed a red baseball cap hanging on a nail. Turning towards a table, in the dim light, she could see that a map was spread out on it. Tytti looked more closely. The map was of the island. It was folded so as to place the castle in the centre. Then, next to the map, something else caught her eye: a recent copy of the *Tapiolinna Times*. It was the edition with the article about the skull.

'And who might you be, then?' A man came slowly forward from a corner of the cabin.

Jumping at the sound of his voice but remaining calm, Tytti replied, 'Just looking for the owner of the boat. Is that you?'

A bald man in a green tracksuit with white stripes down the arms looked her up and down.

'Maybe. Why are you looking for him?'

'So you're not the owner? Then where is he and who are you?'

'Inquisitive, aren't you.'

'And trespassing, aren't you.'

The man laughed. 'Ah, you've got me now.'
They stood, wordlessly, each of them waiting for
the other to divulge more.

'I guess I'll go first then. I'm a private
investigator. I'm looking for a man named Ville
Tapio.'

Tytti looked at him in surprise.

'But Ville Tapio is dead!'

The man gave a gruff laugh.

'Or so you think. I've been hired by a
woman called Anna Tapio, who seems to think
otherwise. So why are *you* snooping around?'

'I was just looking for the owner of the boat.'

The man gave her a hard look.

'Okay, I'm a journalist from the *Tapiolinna
Times*.'

'Listen, maybe we could help each other
then? I don't believe that you should be on this
boat any more than I should. Why are *you*
looking for Ville Tapio?'

'I didn't know I was until now. You see, I
received a tip-off about solving a crime.' She
paused. 'A murder, actually. I thought that
tracking down the tipster would be the best way
to start. I had no idea what else I could do.
Look at this note.'

The PI took Tytti's letter and looked over at
the table. Next to the map was a notepad. A
time and date had been written on it. The PI
compared the handwriting.

'Well, I think we've found your man. So
why does Ville Tapio want you to investigate a

murder? Whose?'

'Well, until now, I thought Ville Tapio was the murder victim!'

How on earth had he come to be alive?

'But now we know that he isn't.' The PI looked at Tytti, debating momentarily whether or not to tell her. 'Anna Tapio says that Ville Tapio has come to the island demanding money. He is the castle arsonist. He burnt down the castle in order to claim the insurance money. It was held in trust, so he could not sell it; there was no other way he could do it. He had run up gambling debts with some very dangerous people and he wanted to disappear, take the money and run. But when Ville Tapio was judged *in absentia*, the castle went to Anna. And despite his threats, she never gave him any money. She hung on to it all, and restored the castle. Ville had to leave the island, as he was officially dead. Now he's back—for his money.'

Money that, although he might come by it illegally, was rightfully his, thought Tytti, unsure of where exactly the fraud began.

'I guess it has something to do with the hotel opening; but Anna refused, and he told her to look out. That he would get his way. And then, after he saw her, he disappeared. He's changed his identity, so she hired me to find him. I'd advise you not to approach him. He's a very dangerous man.'

On the phone, Anna had not sounded surprised

when Tytti had told her she knew that Ville was alive and was the mysterious tipster. The PI must have got there before her. Tytti did not mention how her article on the skull had spread to the tabloids, she was in enough trouble over that already. Then she remembered how unfair that trouble was. Perhaps Anna had been right when she accused Tytti of having no discretion. Maybe it was time for her to develop this skill while continuing her investigation into the skull. Why would Ville Tapio return to the island now, and what was it about the skull in the tree that he was so interested in? And why would he write a tip-off about murdering himself? Had he really burned down the castle and faked his own death?

There was something about the PI's story that did not ring true to Tytti. No — there were too many unanswered questions for her to drop the investigation now.

Chapter Twenty-seven

Teemu's back, thought Tytti as she entered the office and the stench of cigars met her nose.

Teemu's holiday abroad had been overtaken by a revolution. A week of delight followed by closed shops, limited food and boarded-up museums. And all because they had not paid their taxes. Over ten years, they had doubled their salaries but failed to pay their taxes. In Finland that kind of behaviour would wind up with the tax evader being at the very least humiliated and at worst put in prison. There was no leeway for that kind of behaviour. Things were as they should be in Finland when it came to paying tax.

Teemu had confided in Tytti that the thought of going away alone filled him with trepidation; however, he had not been on holiday for a long time, and he had travelled alone as a young man. And for the first week it had been just like five-star backpacking. Isolated in his hotel room for the second week during the revolt, and with time on his hands, he had decided to see if he could get his wife back. This had involved the charming but unoriginal move of sending flowers, lots of flowers.

Now he was back, and since Kai had been

left in charge, Teemu was somewhat nervous about whether he still had a job. Pondering alone, he had begun to realise that he was in fact expendable. He had always viewed himself as a hotshot editor who had once worked at *Helsingin Sanomat*. A person they would not be able to replace in such a far-flung location. But then Kai had come along and, well, replaced him. Now it seemed that an accountant was running the newspaper.

Tytti stood next to Teemu as he sat at his desk. They were discussing the latest developments in his love life. Just before he had gone away he had discovered that his wife's new flame was a yoga instructor she had met on a retreat.

'Some bloke who meditates!' grumbled Teemu. Teemu clicked to cancel his email subscription to the florist he had used to send flowers to his wife. He had had no response from her. His phone beeped. It was a text message from the florist encouraging him to stay subscribed.

'Be sending you flowers soon,' suggested Tytti.

Teemu, angry at the flippant remark, looked at her crossly.

As Tytti went and sat back down at her desk, a dejected-looking Teemu closed his office door. Glancing across at the crown of Kai's golden-blonde head, she wondered what was going on with him. She planned to go and visit

Terhi later, and had mentioned this fact to Kai; but Kai had not seemed particularly enthused about the idea, and Tytti was beginning to wonder if something was wrong. In fact, if she thought back, Kai *had* been treating her rather strangely. Not unfriendly, but, for example, looking at her out of the corner of his eye, and giving terse, non-confrontational answers. He had even stopped making coffee, preferring to nip over to Ritva's for a cup. Although that could be for a whole other reason. Plus he was not looking so good.

He has put on a little weight, thought Tytti, immediately checking her drawer to see if her stash of chocolate was intact. Come to think of it, Ritva looked a bit chubbier than usual too. Wondering about his side of the story, Tytti asked, 'So how did dinner with Ritva, Ulrich and Anna go?'

Kai sat, still in some discomfort from the off perch-pike, and contemplated the question. The dinner had not gone well. His mother had behaved atrociously as usual and expressed a distaste for Ritva; but from Kai's perspective, her behaviour had been satisfactory. As usual Ulrich had been something of a dead weight when it came to conversation, but Ritva had handled it well. It was difficult to read what Ulrich thought about Ritva, but then he was only Kai's godfather. Some might say that Kai was somewhat spoilt by him. Pompous as he could be, Ulrich had a soft spot for Kai and regularly let him borrow his cars, boats or helicopter, his most prized possessions. And although Kai did not appreciate these favours, Ulrich felt he was closer to him than anybody else in his world. Anybody other than his cat (a suspicious tabby stray who had once arrived half-drowned at the sliding glass door of his house in the forest).

'It went well, thank you. I, er, think my mother and Ritva got along quite well.' Kai was too embarrassed to share the truth. He went quiet.

Tytti frowned as she acknowledged his perception, and looked back at her screen. She was trying to bring a new page on science and technology to life but was having trouble finding gadgets relevant to the islanders' lives. Was there really a solar-powered driverless sea limousine? A machine that grows crops and flowers without any soil? It was time for her to look forward through the postmodernist mist and enter this scary world of gadgets.

Tytti pondered about the devices that had already taken over so much of what had once been either manual or unthinkable work. Although she herself was still chopping wood with an axe, and they had been around for millennia.

I guess you just can't beat good old Neolithic design, she mused. Maybe it showed just how little our intelligence had progressed if we could not better a hatchet. Of course, you could buy one these days from a vast selection on the internet.

'A solar-powered sea limousine?' Teemu had appeared at her shoulder.

'We live in an archipelago; a sea limousine would be useful,' said Tytti uncertainly. But what does one really need a solar-powered sea limousine for? she asked herself. A motor-boat would suffice. New technology often struggled to find its place among the old reliable. And the competition was fierce. Solar power was unpopular because the oil, gas and nuclear companies saw to it by bullying their way across the market.

'Dubai might be getting one,' hedged Tytti. 'Their man-made islands are fundamentally similar to our archipelago.'

Teemu looked unconvinced.

'It's controlled by a satellite navigation system,' added Tytti in an encouraging tone.

Teemu pursed his lips.

'And it moves with a hovercraft.' This was her last shot.

'Well... okay. Just don't mention that we might not have enough sunlight to power the thing.'

Teemu returned to his office.

That show wasn't for my benefit, thought Tytti. He was showing Kai who was boss. Putting on a display so Kai knew that he, Teemu, was back in charge.

Chapter Twenty-eight

It was Sunday afternoon. Denis and Tytti were back at the thicket where the silver bar had been discovered way back when. Due to their previous failure, Denis was even more determined to find something and had invested in a second-hand metal detector. A heatwave had hit, and they were sweating. The metal detector crackled and then hummed enticingly.

'Let's dig here!' yelled Denis, at a dip filled with undergrowth where the metal detector had responded. Pulling on his gardening gloves, Denis began to rip up the weeds to make a space to delve. Tytti stood, trowel in hand, ready to kneel down and begin scratching away. Thinking back, Tytti remembered that Denis's interest in archaeology had begun the previous summer, when an ancient grave was discovered in a field next to the graveyard of her father's church. She had mentioned it to Denis and he had spent the long hot summer helping the archaeologists dig for artefacts and remains. When they determined that the grave belonged to an early Finnish Priest, Denis had become hooked. Tytti had never seen him as happy and excited as he had been that summer. She understood his need to work part-time so he could look after his mother who had emphysema, but why was he working as a cleaner at the newspaper? He was a clever young man. And what had happened to his idea of studying archaeology?

'So, how is life with you?' she asked.

'Terrific!' exclaimed Denis. 'I've decided to apply for university to study archaeology next year!' So much that is on one's mind can be in another's, it would seem.

'That's wonderful, Denis!'

'Yes, social services have finally agreed to pay for a carer for my mother.'

Tytti was well aware of the time this decision had taken to be made and the toll that waiting had taken on both Denis and his mother. The guilt she must have felt about holding him back. Nobody wanted to be dependent on the social services. And nobody at social services seemed to be bothered by the delay.

Being reliant on the Finnish social system is like living inside an equation, thought Tytti. The x, perhaps. The Finnish social services were not known for hasty decisions; but once you got one, you could depend on it. A Finnish mind made up was a fortified mind.

'And I'll be able to defer my national service until I've graduated,' said Denis, bringing Tytti's attention back to him.

Tytti had often wondered how army life would agree with Denis. She watched him dig in his Metallica T-shirt, his long hair tied back in a ponytail.

'Actually, I wanted to ask you for a favour… Erm, well, another favour.' Denis felt a little guilty and hoped that Tytti now had more favourable feelings towards excavation.

'Well, er…' said Tytti cautiously. She must remember to tread carefully with Denis.

'Would you, er, possibly be able to, er, write me a recommendation for my university application?'

Tytti heaved a sigh of relief. Writing she could do. And she wanted to do this for Denis.

'Of course I will…' Her words halted as her trowel hit something metal.

Tytti and Denis had found a bullet shell. As soon as she got home, Tytti emailed the ballistics expert she had met when she had once covered a story on a man who had shot his own leg. The man, a biker, had accidentally fired his gun while he had been texting. Now she was hoping to identify the shell case that she and Denis had found.

Sitting back in thought, Tytti was shocked to see a hat walk past the back of her house. Someone was in her garden.

'Excuse me. What are you doing?' asked Tytti of a pair of muddy wellingtons poking out from underneath her gooseberry bush.

She had returned home from the dig hot and sweaty and was now looking forward to a sauna and swim. But first she would have to deal with the man hiding under her gooseberry bush.

The man wriggled backwards towards her, flushed and angry. All his clothing was the same pale khaki as his wellingtons and he held a camera with an enormous lens. With no word of apology and a look of disgust at Tytti's presence, he whispered, 'White-backed woodpecker.' When he waved his GPS phone in her face, she could see some numbers on it which possibly located one of the trees in the vicinity. In her vicinity. Hence the irregular choice of her gooseberry bush for cover. Finland had 'Everyman's Right', and one was free to wander around picking berries and mushrooms; but one of the few rules was to stay away from other people's property. The man did not recognise her — why would he — but Tytti thought there was something familiar about him. Yes: he was the man from the council who had recently been delivering unwanted post to Ritva's bookshop.

'Oh,' she responded, remaining composed but really at a loss for words. 'Carry on then,' and turning, she began to leave him to his stalking of the white-backed woodpecker. Then she stopped and turned around.

'Apologies for asking, but do you have a permit?' Still wriggling under the gooseberry bush, the man's backside and legs could be seen to visibly freeze.

Of course he doesn't have a permit, thought Tytti. Why would he need one to lie down in my garden?

'If you don't, well, then, I'm afraid I'll have to ask you to leave. There's a strict quota on how many people can twitch in this area at one time and only that many permits have been made available.' The man scrabbled out of the bush, his face growing redder and angrier by the second. Then, without a word, he stood up and left.

As Tytti sat naked in the sauna, she chuckled to herself about her run-in with the man from the council. It was only eighty degrees Celsius so she scooped up a ladle of water and flung it on the hot coals. They hissed and the steam rose, nudging the thermometer up a few degrees. She threw on some more water in order to move the dial up to an invigorating ninety, and then lay down on the blistering wooden bench.

'Ahh. Heaven.' There was nothing like a sauna to loosen the muscles and revitalise the mind.

After thirty minutes or so, she was red and sweating. Now was the optimal time to have a swim. She was just hot enough to crave the shocking chill of the sea. Still naked, she walked down the warm stone steps to the small beach next to the jetty. Walking out to sea, she paused as the water reached her knees, the gritty sand swirling between her toes, and felt the cool breeze tousle her hair. She continued to wade out to sea, and then launched herself into the water, the sudden cold cooling her hot body.

Head bobbing above the water, she began to swim. When she reached a good distance out, she turned over onto her back and, looking up into the flawless blue sky, lay floating in the shape of a star.

Peacefully, lazily, she watched the inverted islands of the archipelago rise and twist, with humps and bumps, like a great coiled sea monster with green tree-scales and grey granite skin, gently resting in its ice-age slumber. She looked to see if there was anybody swimming near the opposite island. One would occasionally see a white bottom now and again from a nude picnicker.

Bliss, thought Tytti. This is just how life should be.

Back on shore, wearing a dressing gown and with a towel wrapped around her head, she began to arrange things ready to watch the Perseid shower that was due to rain down that night: white sparks falling in a dark sky, darting at all angles, tails trailing behind. Tonight, she would be staying up: cocooned in a sleeping bag and reclining on a sun lounger, she would repose on the jetty and watch the torrent of meteors cascade over the jet-black sea. Watching the meteors had been a custom for her and Henri. With a flask full of coffee they had always stayed awake as long as possible and watched the dazzling sky.

Well, I'll have plenty of shooting stars to

wish upon, thought Tytti happily.

She was partly doing this in memory of him. Watching the falling stars reminded her of their love. Gentle and encompassing. That feeling inside, of affection and excitement, when she knew she was going to see him.

Maybe her father was right. The situation with her boyfriend had hardened her. Perhaps it was time for her to move on. Time to rewrite her memories.

Chapter Twenty-nine

The sun shone through the small-paned window and into her eyes, waking her far earlier than she would have chosen. The previous night, she had fallen asleep in the sun lounger and only been awoken when drops of rain had begun to fall on her face. Now the summer rain had ceased and beads of water on the surface of every green plant magnified the light, causing her to squint as she took a deep breath of fresh air from the open window.

Once dressed and outside, she wiped the raindrops off her saddle and handlebars with a threadbare towel that still pictured a faded Moomintroll. The dirt-and-gravel lane leading from her house was peppered with muddy puddles, and so, in order to save her white ankle socks from dirty splashes, she pushed her bicycle along beside her, through the cool fresh forest and into a fuzzy beam of warm sunlight. In the still air hung the scent of cow parsley and wild rose. Gnats swirled frantically, never leaving some unknown perimeter.

When she reached the main road, it looked free from filth so she mounted her bicycle and pushed off. There was very little traffic and

Tytti whistled to herself as she rode along in something of a daze, her knees growing pleasantly warm, newly bathed in the sun.

All of a sudden, a car appeared alongside her.

Landing heavily on her shoulder, Tytti fell through nettles and long grass into the wet ditch. Disrupted by her landing, a blast of nettle pollen brought a sharp sneeze to her nose and scads of dandelion seeds enveloped her.

Tytti pulled herself up and leant against a dead tree that had not a scrap of bark left on it, and roots covered in wormholes. Rubbing her shoulder, she could see that her arms and legs were scratched all over from the brambles. Then she saw a head and heard a voice. A wizened brown face peered down at her.

'Hello,' said the old man, with some amusement.

'Hello,' replied Tytti.

'Can I give you a hand?'

The old man wore a blue Mao cap. In one hand he carried a bunch of pussy willow: light-brown velvet mittens tacked to a stick, saluting upwards at evenly spaced intervals. First, he pulled Tytti out before straightening her bicycle.

'See, no harm done,' he said kindly. Tytti rubbed her arm.

'Did you see the car that tried to hit me?'

'Only that it was black. I was busy collecting pussy willow.'

Tytti slid back onto her bicycle and resumed

her ride along the wet road.

Shaken by her close encounter, Tytti walked unsteadily over to the bookshop. She pushed the door, but it was jammed. Putting her sore shoulder to the frame, she pushed harder. Nothing. It was locked. Ritva knew that Tytti often came by before work, but this time she had locked her out. Or could the man from the council have finally had enough and closed Ritva down? Unlikely. It hadn't yet been four weeks, the time Ritva had been allocated to apply for the permit to run the coffee shop. Then she saw Lili scratching at the door and knew for sure that Ritva had simply shut her out.

It must be because of what I said to Terhi, thought Tytti. Had she really expected no fallout? Naively: yes. Whereas she herself had forgotten all about it. Maybe Terhi had put it across in the wrong way? But Terhi was straight to the point and unlikely to exaggerate such a thing.

So Ritva had turned against her. And it was Tytti's own fault. Kai must have finished it with her when he had learned of her unscrupulous motives. That must have been what had happened.

'Morning,' said Teemu, sneering somewhat as Tytti walked in. This was the last thing she needed. Kai had neither looked up nor said good morning. The atmosphere in the office was decidedly hostile. Choosing to ignore Teemu, she said good morning to Kai and then went into the kitchen and opened the first-aid cabinet for the antihistamine cream. That would ease her suffering.

'A word, Tytti.' Teemu was standing by the kitchen door.

Still trying to be the boss, thought Tytti with a sigh. The cream would have to wait.

She followed Teemu as he returned to his office and sat down at his desk. Tapping his mouse, his screen saver disappeared and a website was revealed.

'Come and look at this.' Tytti stood behind him and read over his shoulder.

'*A Bridge to Understanding.*' It was the website for the yoga teacher's studio. '*Have you ever thought of this "thing" called "oneness"? Have you ever thought that, to truly experience yourself, you need to create a world of separate, independent yous? Each one reflecting the all of who you are…*'

A possibility, thought Tytti — but why was Teemu showing her this?

'This,' declared Teemu, 'is who my wife has left me for. Someone who writes horseshit about "independent yous". I know which one of the independent yous this bloke is after. How could my wife have left me for someone like that? If anyone should have left, it should have been me!' said Teemu. Their sex life had been somewhat abysmal for a while. Doing the same old thing, which worked, but it was just the same old thing. Maybe this yogi had some tricks up his sleeve. It did not even cross Teemu's mind that his wife might have gone to be with the man for the very qualities that he, Teemu, despised him for. Gentleness, openness… maybe she was with him for the way he made her feel.

Tytti returned to her desk, amused, and noticed a miserable-looking Kai along the way. She saw him staring at a spreadsheet on his computer, seemingly unmotivated to shift any numbers about. He was blankly staring at a brick wall of rows, columns and cells. A mini prison on his screen.

Feeling a twinge of pity, Tytti asked, 'How are you today?'

'Bad,' said Kai.

'And what might the matter be?'

Kai looked up at her. His gaze was firm.

'It's okay to say it, Tytti. We both of us have realised it.'

'Realised what?' asked Tytti.

'And it's okay for you to admit it.'

Okay, he wants me to apologise for not talking to him directly.

'You're jealous.'

'What?'

'It's okay, though. We've talked about it, and Ritva has explained your history to me, how you've been unable to find a boyfriend since your old boyfriend died.'

'She said what!' Tytti was affronted at having her intimate conversations with Ritva repeated as hearsay.

'Oh, yes, she explained in detail.'

Kai's usual upbeat attitude had taken a battering, and all because of Tytti. After Terhi had relayed Tytti's opinion, a sit-down with Ritva had resulted in Ritva persuading Kai that Tytti was just jealous. Hence Tytti had lied and said that Ritva was only after his money and status. And although Ritva had told him not to mention it to Tytti, he felt that she should know so that she could work on this area of her personality. Honesty, no matter how misplaced, was also Kai's best policy.

Chapter Thirty

After a slow workday filled with awkward silences, Tytti was relieved to be home. It was a still evening, with a calm sea. Tytti remembered that she must check the wire baskets in the water; yesterday there had been no fish, but today there might be a small pike or perch, a bit bony but still good to eat. Outside, she went down the stairs to where the sea lapped at the jetty. She bent down and pulled the twine that secured her basket to a wooden post. It was empty. It was time to go fishing.

The first chore was to use an old ice-cream container to bail out the rainwater from the scratched white rowing boat. Then, with rolled up trousers and bare muddy feet, she pushed the boat through the shallows. It had been sitting at an angle in the mire, and she had to push hard to get it through the reeds. She walked through the silted water until it became deep enough for the boat to float unaided, and then climbed in.

As she rowed out to sea, the wooden oars felt rough against her clasped palms. One of the rowlocks was slightly looser than the other, forcing her to row unevenly in order to keep the boat straight. One stroke here, a stroke and a bit there. But this was something she was used to and which added to the touch.

The further she rowed, the blacker the water became and the smoother on top. As she reached the deep water, she twisted the oars up into the boat and waited for it to settle. She picked up the long, silver birch branch she used as a fishing rod — a simple bough with a line tied to the end. She fed a worm onto the hook and cast off. Hunched forward, with her knees together, she prepared herself to watch the red and white bobber.

The sun stroked her faded yellow hat and she began to think about her life and the situation she was in. Everything seemed to be up in the air. There had yet to be any news from Dr Wahlroos about the skull in the tree, and Tytti herself had been unable to find out anything more about it. No information had come back about the bullet yet either.

Then there was Ritva and Kai. After his outburst, Kai had not spoken to Tytti for the rest of the day, and she had been too embarrassed to return to the subject. Foolishly, Kai believed Ritva's story about Tytti being jealous of their relationship. Checkmate for Ritva. There was now very little Tytti could do to break them up without appearing to have an ulterior motive.

A tug on the line, and the bobber flashed in the water. Forgetting about her predicament, Tytti struck and pulled her first fish out. Three fish later, she felt restless. Ville Tapio was on her mind. She picked up the oars. It was time for her to row over to the castle and speak to Anna.

Chapter Thirty-one

Seated once again in Anna's office at the castle, Tytti asked, 'Wasn't it a terrible shock when he reappeared?'

'It was something I'd dreaded for years. I had even hoped that something had happened to Ville, if you know what I mean. That would have saved a lot of heartache.'

'What do you mean "heartache"?'

Anna frowned, went over to a window and banged it shut.

'You have to tell me if I'm going to be able to help you,' Tytti added.

'If I tell you this, you must swear to keep it secret. Can you do that for me Tytti?'

'Yes, of course,' said Tytti quickly.

'There was an accident that took place many years ago, thirty or so years ago. The accident that cost Heike his life.'

'It's okay, I know that he drowned while out ice fishing. The ice cracked and he went under.' She felt there was no need for Anna to relay such a sad tale.

'Yes,' said Anna, 'Yes, that is what everybody thinks. But that is not what happened.'

The door was closed, and Anna was seated

at her desk. Tytti sat opposite, listening intently.

'Oh God!' exclaimed Anna. 'Nobody knows this except Ville and I! Well, that's what I thought, until now.'

'Just take your time. There's no need to rush.'

Anna took a deep breath.

'I had just discovered that I was pregnant with Heike's child. When I told Ville, instead of him being happy about it, he broke down in tears. It turned out he was in love with me and had been biding his time before he told me. I guess it makes sense, twins falling in love with the same woman. Anyway, Ville was an emotional wreck. He went to confront Heike about his feelings for me. He ran out of the castle and down to the sea where Heike was fishing through a hole in the ice. I followed as quickly as I could, but by the time I got there they were already arguing. Then the argument became physical. Ville started to shove Heike in order to make him fight, and soon they were locked in each other's grip, trying to grapple each other to the ground.

And that was when Heike slipped. He slipped and fell, hitting his head on the auger he had used to cut the ice. As he went down, he pulled Ville on top of him. There was a look of surprise on both of their faces. I think Heike was dead as soon as he landed. A huge ugly gash in the back of his head. We couldn't believe it.'

Anna sat quietly, reliving the scene in her

mind.

'Is that when you pushed him into the sea?'

'No!' Anna looked devastated. 'Ville was losing control. He kept saying that they would blame him for Heike's death. That he would be put in prison for murder. I tried to tell him that he wouldn't, that things would be all right if we just went to the police and explained what had happened. God, we were only teenagers! But Ville decided that we had to hide Heike's body. He said we couldn't drop him in the sea in case he came up and they found the wound on his head.' Anna shuddered. 'He became methodical in his search for a solution. Asked me to help him bury Heike. I refused, and that was when he turned on me. He took my arm and bent it behind my back. He fractured it. I couldn't go to the doctor. He would have asked too many questions. It has never been the same since — see.'

Anna held up her right hand. It shook slightly.

'Oh, Tytti, I was so scared for my life, and the life of my child. He said he would tell the police that I had helped him to murder Heike, that I would go to prison along with him. My baby would be born in prison and be taken away from me. So I agreed. But it was winter and the ground was frozen. Then Ville had the idea of burying Heike over in the bog. The land up there freezes later than the rest of the ground. Ville put the body on a sledge and I helped him to push it there.

'The bog overgrown by the copse? Where Denis and I have been digging for silver?'

'Have you? I wasn't aware.'

Tytti was dumbstruck. The site where she and Denis had been digging was where Heike's body lay. A coincidence, and a strange one. Anna paused.

'I think Ville has been digging up there too. Did you know?'

'I did wonder if he might try. He thinks that the person who put the skull in the tree knows about the accident and is taunting us. He wants to find the body and destroy it. No body — no crime.'

Chapter Thirty-two

It was only ten to four when Ritva decided her workday was complete. She walked over to the shop door and locked it. Outside, a middle-aged man waved frantically at her, pointing to his watch.

'Closed,' she said, forcefully pulling down the blind. After all the missed phone calls and text messages from Tytti, Ritva had finally reached the point where she was ready to talk to her. She wanted to know why Tytti had betrayed her.

Tytti waited apprehensively at the outdoor market café. The grey cobblestones shone, newly washed, while rainwater dripped from the edges of the white canvas marquee. She had been about to give up when Ritva had sent her a text message suggesting they meet here.

'A nice, polite text message,' thought Tytti. That was a good start.

Her mind drifted to the pending apology. What was she going to say? Taking her time, Tytti began to think long and hard. Perhaps as long and hard as the Finnish winter. Sometimes she thought a Finnish solution to a problem was a sign of this long, cold season. Shut away indoors with so much time to think; finding answers to questions which might have been better left unanswered. Trying to catch the mistake before it happened. But yes, most solutions to most problems only caused another problem. It was a constant patching-up job. Some mistakes went on for far too long—each bad decision patched up with another bad decision. At times a person just ought to say, 'Sorry, I was wrong. I have made a horrible mess of the economy/the dinner/your haircut—please forgive me,' and move on, in the hope that the other person would as well.

Extracting herself from her analysis, Tytti decided she could still not quite bring herself to make a full apology. But then, out of the blue, she thought about her father and what he would counsel in this situation. She would try harder, for his sake. Yes, apologising was an uncomfortable social skill that most people had learned to forget. Maybe they just did not see the initial wrong. It was all just a difference of opinion rather than a disagreement. And blame and anger were easier to pin on someone else than oneself.

Maybe she should reward herself for the realisation that she had made a mistake.

Tytti spotted Ritva coming from the other side of the market. She was, as always, wearing a multitude of colours.

'Good afternoon. How are you?' began

Ritva as she arrived.

'Thank you, good. And how are you?'

'Not bad, thank you.' Then there was silence.

'This stall sells some very good cinnamon buns. Shall I get two?' suggested Tytti, hoping a peace offering would put her in a favourable position. But really she knew that Ritva was expecting more than food. She was waiting for Tytti to be contrite.

'I'll go,' said Ritva, who was closer to the counter.

Ritva returned with two coffees and placed everything on the red-and-white checked tablecloth. Seagulls were screaming and wheeling around their heads, hoping for a bite.

'I'm sorry,' said Tytti quietly, looking down at the table.

Ritva sat in silence. Then she said, 'What are you sorry for, Tytti?'

Tytti was surprised.

'Well, I'm sorry for telling Terhi my opinion of your and Kai's relationship.' Even at this delicate stage she still felt she had to tell the truth.

Ritva sighed. Tytti had, after all, been telling the truth.

'And I'm sorry for telling Kai that you were secretly in love with him.'

Secretly in love! Kai had not mentioned that.

Ritva looked awkward.

'Yes, I might have overstated it a bit. I know you like him a lot.'

Ritva paused. Telling Tytti the truth was harder than she'd expected. She began to realise what a phony she must have seemed in pretending to like Kai. But now she *had* grown to like him. But would Tytti believe her, even though it was the truth?

'You see, well, Kai has grown on me. I do actually like him quite a lot. And I think he likes me.'

Tytti wondered if Ritva was being honest. She must be becoming a good liar to have tricked Kai and then managed to spin a story about her. But in the past Ritva had been honest. Could one man really change all that? Tytti found herself wondering if they had slept together yet. Maybe Ritva had a plan for that too. A scheme to make sure she became a Tapio? Get him drunk, not too drunk, just drunk enough, and use her feminine charms to get him into bed. Even a phantom pregnancy would be enough to set the papers talking, perhaps even leading to a shotgun wedding. Just look at what had happened between that prince and the Olympic skater. A sham of a marriage — but she had become a princess anyway.

Tytti stopped. Ritva was looking at her rather quizzically.

'Let's just drop the whole thing,' said Tytti quickly.

Ritva was glad to comply. They would never be in full agreement on this subject, so whitewashing it seemed the best option — each one ignoring the faults of the other, as only good friends can.

Chapter Thirty-three

As Tytti cycled over to the vicarage, she mentally took notes for the report she would be writing: '… severe thunderstorm — hailstones the size of golf balls…' and possibly '… streets flooded for a time — a fire caused by lightning…' then, unusually '… worst storm for 30 years…'

She had been thinking about her father and his usually sage advice. Now she needed it. She arrived just as the thunderstorm hit, to find the vicarage already without power. An angry bolt of lightning struck just as Tytti entered the hall. Candles around the living room cast a warm and welcoming light into the corners. Her father had taken the landline off the hook due to the possibility of lightning striking a telephone pole. Tytti took off her shoes and then went to sit down in the living room. Her father was hovering next to the window, watching the rain flatten his flowers.

He's probably wondering what cake to give me, thought Tytti. He seemed distant, and had not yet offered any sustenance. She wondered why her father was lingering at the window and not sitting down.

'Dad, er…' Sitting here in this cosy room made what she was about to say sound ridiculous. 'I think someone is trying to threaten or maybe even kill me.'

Risto looked at her in astonishment. Then he laughed. He was well aware of his daughter's impressive imagination.

Tytti frowned. She had not expected this from her father. When a daughter tells a father that someone is trying to kill them, he should, at least, look concerned. Instead, he looked, well, distracted.

'And I'm not exaggerating or making this up,' stressed Tytti. 'I had somebody try to asphyxiate me and then try to run me over.'

'Tytti. Tytti. Would someone really try to asphyxiate you? To run you over?' He turned his head to watch his flowers again.

Her father was not taking her seriously. He had not even asked her how the incidents had occurred. Maybe if she explained more clearly.

'Are you sure you're not being paranoid?' interjected Risto. He wondered if these imaginings were a symptom of her losing faith in people.

'I think it might be Anna Tapio,' said Tytti quietly.

Risto looked at Tytti in bewilderment.

'But why would Anna want to kill you? What on earth could you have done, Tytti?'

Nothing to deserve that! thought Tytti. And why was her father so sceptical? Did he like Anna enough to defend her against his own daughter? Strange as it seemed, Tytti suddenly wondered if her father was in love with Anna.

There was a knock on the door.

'Coffee's ready.' It was Miina.

They both went into the kitchen. On the table rested three cups of coffee. Tytti had hoped to find her father alone, but Miina had been there. The two women avoided eye contact. They were yet to become friendly.

'Who would like cake?' Risto noted the tension and tried to buoy up the atmosphere with an encouraging voice.

'No, thank you,' said Tytti and Miina in unison.

'Are you sure?' Risto asked, offended. It was unusual for a Finn to refuse a slice of cake. Especially one freshly baked by himself. Being such a popular vicar, he usually had to make eight or so birthday cakes, wanting a piece for any visitor who dropped by to wish him well. As a result, he had become rather a good baker. Opening his mouth to offer a biscuit, Tytti cut in.

'You said you were planning to move to the island? When will this be?'

'Soon. Perhaps in the next month or so,' replied Miina cordially. There was an awkward silence. Risto got a grip of himself.

'There is actually something you need to know.' Risto cleared his throat. 'Miina used to be a… er… a… er…' Risto struggled to end the sentence.

'… a prostitute.' Miina ended the sentence for him. The word hung in the air.

Tytti swallowed hard, but did not flinch. She considered her father and Miina and could see how happy they were. Miina's past meant nothing to them. She could have said she had been a hairdresser. Tytti continued, 'And where do you intend on living?'

I'm proud of you, Risto thought relieved. His daughter had grown up to be non-judgemental.

Risto and Miina glanced at each other.

'Well... actually, we have some more news for you. We've decided to get married!' Risto went over to Miina and placed his hand on her shoulder.

'Married!'

'Indeed, Tytti, married.'

'But, why...' Tytti stopped as she grasped why. The appropriate thing for a vicar to do was to be married. To not live in sin.

'Well... congratulations,' mumbled Tytti, feeling more shocked than pleased at this revelation over the previous one. She was used to having her dad to herself. Since her mother had died, he had not had a relationship; it had been just the two of them. Tytti had expected things to stay that way. 'Have you spoken to the Synod yet?' Getting married was the decent thing to do, but what would the religious community think about Miina's past life?

'Yes, I've told the bishop. He bestowed his blessing upon us.

'Have you told him the whole story?'

'No, not yet,' said Risto cheerfully.

'But dad, you have to inform the church. The truth has a funny way of coming out.'

'But what would they think?' Miina said in a low voice.

'They'll probably think it unconventional but acceptable,' predicted Tytti. 'It's not like you've been throwing Christians to the lions or anything.' Tytti's joke fell flat.

'Well, if you think it's what we should do, let's tell the bishop first and see how he reacts.' Risto had begun to look concerned. Miina turned and gazed up at him.

'Yes,' she said. 'Yes, I think it's the proper thing to do.'

The doorbell rang. Risto went to answer it. Tytti had a million questions, but sat in silence. Constable Mansikka-aho followed Risto back into the room. He looked embarrassed.

'Well, I'm afraid that this is a formal visit. Are you Pauliina?' asked Constable Mansikka-aho, looking towards Miina. Miina nodded, almost imperceptibly. 'In that case, I'm going to have to arrest you, Risto.'

'Dad?' Tytti asked sharply. And then, to Constable Mansikka-aho: 'Why are you arresting my father?'

The policeman started to redden, but answered Tytti's question.

'Because your father has been soliciting.'

Tytti gasped in amazement and looked over to her father.

'Officer, there has been some kind of mix-up. You see, Pauli… I mean Miina is just here to drop off some collection money.'

'Are you aware that she is a prostitute?' The description hung hard in the air.

'Well, er, yes… It's just… Oh, well, we have been seeing each other, yes—but as partners in a relationship. This is all a silly mix-up.'

'Well, then, we can clear up the confusion down at the police station, can't we.'

The policeman put out his hand and gestured for Risto to leave before him.

Chapter Thirty-four

Once the storm had abated, Tytti cycled hastily over to the castle. As she climbed the stairs to Suvi-Tuuli's studio, her mind wandered back to the last time she had been there. She remembered painting a picture of a seagull. A childish attempt, which nonetheless had been tacked to the wall of her bedroom by her proud father. She knocked on the door. She could hear Suvi-Tuuli sniff on the other side; she did not bother to answer the knock. Maybe she was busy working? Tytti knocked again, then put her ear to the door. She could hear Suvi-Tuuli shuffling about. Maybe she didn't want to see anyone. Tytti rattled the door, and followed up with a more insistent knock. She was not going away, so Suvi-Tuuli might as well answer. But she still did not. Before Tytti knew quite what she was doing, she had pushed the door open and placed herself in front of Suvi-Tuuli.

Suvi-Tuuli stood, lost in thought, cleaning a paintbrush next to a paint-stained sink. Slowly putting down the paintbrush, she wondered what had taken Tytti so long to come in search of answers.

'Come in my dear, come in,' she said with a warm tone to her voice. 'I was wondering when you would find time to visit me. A silly old lady like me can't be at the top of your list.' She was busy enjoying the blend of turpentine and rose-scented soap on the air.

Unprepared for such a warm reception since she had just barged straight in, Tytti was caught off-guard. Sometimes there seemed to be a discrepancy between what she expected Suvi-Tuuli to do and what she actually did. Suvi-Tuuli seemed to be changing, right before her very eyes.

'I hope you don't mind my dropping in,' replied Tytti in her nicest voice. Two could play at this game.

'Well, people are interested in my art, but very few seem to make it over to see it anymore.'

Gazing around her, Tytti saw the same scene displayed over and over again. Some versions were sketches, some miniatures; but her eye was held by a large oil-painted canvas.

'Yes, this is my masterpiece. I've been working on it for three years. Would you like to take a photograph of it, perhaps with me standing beside it?'

The painting was enormous, taller than Tytti herself. A paint-spattered stepladder stood next to it.

'Well, Kai has taken over the photography.'

An angry shadow crossed Suvi-Tuuli's face.

'Well, I've just finished it. Literally. Just signed it before you came in.' She had written her name in large letters across the bottom of the painting. 'Would you care for some tea? I never drink coffee.' Suvi-Tuuli continued to talk as she crossed the studio to a little kitchen. She switched on the kettle, then looked back at Tytti, waiting for her answer.

'Yes, that would be lovely.'

'I have several herbal teas that you might like.'

What the hell was she doing? Tytti was beginning to wonder if Suvi-Tuuli was not a little bit mad. Unable to think of any small talk, she waded straight in.

'My mother. You alluded to her at the hotel opening. I was wondering what you meant by the things you said. You said it was good that my mother died when she did, and that I should forgive my father?'

'Well now,' said Suvi-Tuuli with a smile. 'That would have been terribly bold of me. I'm sure I said no such thing.' The old woman reached forward and moved the stepladder away from the canvas. Protecting her creation.

'But you did... you *did*,' insisted Tytti, beginning to feel like a child who has misunderstood something fundamental. She began to feel vulnerable: she had come for answers, and was now being denied even the questions.

Suvi-Tuuli closed one eye and looked critically at her great painting. Then she went over to a smaller canvas that was sitting on an easel to be primed. She picked up a brush, dipped it into the white, paint-like primer, and began a second coat.

'Yes, your mother, she did die young. It was terribly sad,' said Suvi-Tuuli. 'So, she and your father met when, exactly?'

'At a dance. They both liked to dance.'

'And we all know what those dances were a cover for. Did your mother understand what she was getting into?'

'What do you mean, "getting into"?'

'Your father was a vicar then, wasn't he? But he was also a man. And we all know what men are like. What they want. And how they sometimes get it, with broken promises. Then, of course, there is the switching of partners. Trying each one on for size, so to speak. Are you absolutely sure that your father is who he says he is?'

Tytti stood very still.

'Yes, your mother was weak to give in to him. It was a shock to us all when they had to rush into the wedding.'

Was that it? wondered Tytti. Her parents had had sex before marriage. Her mother had been pregnant when she married her father. A shameful state of affairs to Suvi-Tuuli, but not to Tytti. She had a more natural attitude. Babies will be born whenever they are ready.

'And how is Risto these days? Has he met anybody else yet? Unusual for a man to be alone for so long. Unnatural really.'

'He wasn't alone. He was with me.'

'Hopefully not in the biblical sense,' laughed Suvi-Tuuli, exposing small yellowed teeth.

What is *wrong* with her? wondered Tytti. She sounds so bitter. And then, suddenly, she realised. She understood that Suvi-Tuuli was digging for dirt and knew nothing about her parents' marriage. She did not actually have any answers about the situations she was alluding to.

Tytti looked more closely at her. For the first time she noticed the bulldog-like set of Suvi-Tuuli's jaw. And it was now that she noticed a framed photograph of a class of schoolgirls of around fourteen, all wearing long black dresses that covered their arms and which went down to their ankles. Dresses that would have been worn at the old Lutheran girls' school on the island. And Suvi-Tuuli was in the picture, wearing a large crucifix.

Putting down the paintbrush, Suvi-Tuuli took out and opened a packet of tobacco and began to fill a clay pipe.

'And why have you been writing threatening letters to your own daughter?' Tytti demanded. 'Your signature on your landscape — it's the same writing as in the letters she received.'

'What letters?' Suvi-Tuuli gave Tytti a look of disbelief. Then Tytti thought of the photographs Kai had taken.

'The evening of the hotel opening. You can see the oak tree from your studio.'

'Yes, I can see the oak tree.'

'Did you see anybody hanging around? Anyone who could have put the skull into the tree?'

She waved a burning match and lit up her clay pipe.

'Now, why would I notice a thing like that?'

'So, you are sure that you did not put it there? You have a ladder.'

Suvi-Tuuli blinked and gave Tytti a surprised glance.

'Now, why on earth would I do such a thing?'

'To scare Anna, for some reason.'

'I don't know what you're talking about. Now get out and leave me alone!'

Chapter Thirty-five

Tytti tapped 'end' on her phone and continued to push her bicycle up the muddy hill. She wondered what to do. After a brief interview, her father had been released by the police without charge. Constable Mansikka-aho had believed his explanation, that Miina was there as his partner and not as a sex worker. An awkward conversation at the most relaxed of times, but even more so when both were wearing their official garments — a dog collar and a police uniform. Luckily, only the four of them knew of the situation. Well, that was as far as Tytti knew. But could there be somebody else, who had tipped off the police?

Tytti pondered what to do, though she already knew the answer; she went through the philosophical motions only for her own peace of mind. The story of a local vicar being arrested for soliciting should have been front-page news — and a splash that could fail to present the error of his arrest until the following edition. A week of having his reputation called into question, after years of trust from the islanders. But no — he was her father. A man she loved, despite their frequent clashes of opinion. She was no turncoat. She would lie about the event by omission.

Tytti was almost up the hill when her phone rang again.

'Oh, Tytti! There's been an accident. The helicopter crashed. Both Kai and Ulrich were in it!'

Before Tytti could absorb this information and ask questions, Ritva continued, 'By some miracle they are both alive, although hurt. They're already in the hospital. It seems the helicopter had been due to land and was only ten or so metres from the ground when Ulrich lost control.'

Tytti swallowed hard.

'How badly hurt are they?'

'I'm just off to the hospital to find out. Are you coming?'

Bonded by calamity, they both rushed to Kai's side.

Ulrich sat propped up in bed. Unlike Kai's room, adorned with flowers and a balloon from his younger siblings, Ulrich's was bare except for a glass of water on the bedside table. Through the open door, Tytti could see that Ulrich was in a lot of pain. Pausing from following Ritva, she went in, moved the visitor's chair and quietly sat down next to the bed.

'How are you?' she asked softly. He had a large plaster and bandage around his head. Ulrich slowly opened his eyes. Tytti could see they were sticky and glazed. He seemed to be heavily medicated.

For the pain, thought Tytti. The poor man. She felt a rush of sympathy.

Ulrich gazed at her and mumbled something. Tytti could not make out what he said. She leaned forward to hear him better.

'I nearly killed him.' He slurred his words.

'No, you never nearly killed someone, you had an accident, an accident in the helicopter,' said Tytti gently. She did not know how much he remembered. He had plainly suffered a blow to the head. Then she thought for a second. The indulged Kai. The penchant for fennel. She gasped at the words.

'I nearly killed my son.'

Ulrich clearly mistook her for somebody else, or was so drugged up that he would disclose such intimate information to anybody. They had never really spoken before, despite being in each other's orbit, especially on such confidential subjects.

Ulrich Tollet, the silent watcher of Kai. Always ready to jump in and defend him from Anna when she needed to be taken in hand. Ulrich was CEO of an investment bank in Stockholm. His wife lived in Stockholm and was the major shareholder of this bank and, as such, could appoint the CEO. And she did not want a divorce. So the union continued although the marriage was long dead. They had both sought solace elsewhere. Ulrich with Anna, although their affair had started long before his marriage had become a farce. That was what people did not know. It had started just before Anna married Simo. Simo had become the patsy when Ulrich had got Anna pregnant.

Ulrich's marriage was the worst-kept secret around, but as he was such a powerful man nobody dared to mention it. Kai always thought that Ulrich was interested in his mother and that was why he hung around. He never realised that they had a history and that Ulrich put up with Anna so that he could see Kai. Secrets had been kept. Kai had always ungratefully expected favours from Ulrich, his supposed godfather. And Ulrich liked to spoil Kai. Along with the motorbikes and cars, he had even given him a sought-after job at the bank. Put him in a place where he could have contact with him. He also kept up his affair with Anna, a difficult person at the best of times, cemented so there was no way he could be cut off from Kai.

Tytti looked around as a doctor arrived and picked up the notes clipped to the end of the bed. Ulrich closed his eyes.

'We were in the army together,' said the doctor amiably. 'Relieved they survived the crash and there wasn't just a pink mist.'

'What happened?' asked Tytti.

'It seems that the grandmother complained about the helicopter ruining her view and told them to move it, to land it on the other side of the island. The side with strong crosswinds. Despite Ulrich being a new pilot, he managed to get the helicopter down, although it was more of a crash than a landing.'

Tytti watched Ulrich. He no longer seemed aware of her presence.

Chapter Thirty-six

Deep in thought, Tytti plotted her attack. The previous morning Denis had been cleaning the office when Tytti had come in. Surprised he was there so late in the day, she realised he was waiting for her and immediately guessed why. Now, she considered the conversation they had had.

'You didn't get in, did you?' gasped Tytti. She had been so sure his application would make it.

'No, I didn't. I can't believe this has happened. I've waited so long. Now I'll have to go into the army.' He took a piece of paper from his pocket and passed it to Tytti. It was the rejection letter.

Tytti had immediately felt guilty. Could it be because of the reference she wrote, that Denis had not got in? Denis looked up at her; there was blame in his eyes. She felt horrible. Because of the reference — the truthful reference she had written — Denis had not been admitted to university. Should she have been less honest and exaggerated the positive aspects of his character? Clearly yes — but what positive aspects?

Tytti read the rejection letter. Looking to the

end, she could see it came from a Dr Anseli Aho.

Well, Dr Anseli Aho, she thought, this isn't over yet. Maybe there was a way to convince Aho that Denis was a good enough bet.

Deep in thought she continued her Sunday hike around the island. Usually, Ritva would have been there with her, but she had chosen to spend the day nursing Kai. Surrounded by long grasses and lean silver birch, the pink gravel path crunched rhythmically, as Tytti hiked along. She loved the long, hot summers when the night sun hovered beneath the horizon, and it never really became dark. Saunas and swimming in the sea. The path began to narrow, ascending through a thickening forest, a forest dense with elm, sycamore and conifer. The trail then changed direction and rose steeply again towards a split rock face of bruised blues and reds, like a silverside of beef, and then to a ridge of rock where a few scanty Scots pines grew. She could hear the sea now. Glittering stars twinkled on a vast maze of water threading among the surrounding islands. She felt the warm breeze on her face, relaxed and enjoyed nature's triumph in wonder.

On a day like this, there were many people, children and dogs up there enjoying their leisure time.

'Good morning,' said Tytti, standing aside to let a family with young children pass along the ridge.

'Good morning!' they all replied in unison,

even the toddler managing something.

'Good morning,' said Tytti to a man coming from the other direction. The man utterly ignored her.

Tytti looked over her shoulder and watched him walk away from her.

Could it be? The picture she had seen in the newspaper cutting about the Tapio family. The portrait of Heike and Anna Tapio. This man looked just like Heike. This man was Heike's twin. *It was Ville Tapio.* Tytti gasped and paused, unsure of what to do. Was this not her opportunity to confront him about starting the fire at the castle? Faking his own death? But why did he think that a murder had taken place? What else did he know? This was her break. She quickly turned around and walked back along the path, ready to confront him; but there was no sign of him.

She looked towards the forest. There was a line of broken twigs and brambles. Somebody had walked into the forest. Then it hit her — where she was: exactly at the place where Denis had finished searching that first time they had come to the copse. Yes, a disappointed Denis had looked over the precipice at exactly that point, the highest point. Was the broken undergrowth merely the traces she and Denis had left when they had exited the forest that day?

No, thought Tytti, he has entered the forest. She looked towards the dark and musty woodland, a gap of broken ferns, and then darkness. Ville Tapio must have been the man Denis had seen that day up at the copse. It seemed his intuition may have been right when he had chosen not to follow him.

Well, curiosity may have killed the cat, thought Tytti, but I... am not a cat.

She turned resolutely towards the forest.

Inside the copse, the sound of the sea was deadened by the thick undergrowth. Tytti stood still and listened carefully. She could hear a scratching sound. Then it stopped. Then it began again. Stop... start. No, not a squirrel withdrawing to a treetop, that was easy to recognise; this sound was more forceful. This was the sound of a shovel. Ville was somewhere through the trees ahead of her, digging. Carefully she walked forward, trying not to snap the undergrowth, and grateful for the regular scraping of the shovel. Then she heard a cough and realised just how close Ville Tapio must be.

Quickly, she hunkered down among some tree roots, crouching in a hollow, a place where once a bear might have slept. As her breathing calmed, Tytti's thoughts began to compose themselves. Why was she hiding? Very likely Ville did not want to be discovered. Then the words of the PI echoed in her head: Ville Tapio is a very dangerous man.

Tytti thought about it for a minute or two, tossing good and bad scenarios across her mind.

The best course of action seemed to be to declare her existence. She rose to her knees, but as she straightened up the ground beneath her began to sink. The earth began to crumble, sucking Tytti down, feet first.

Chapter Thirty-seven

Slapping her hand across her mouth to stop herself from screaming, she plummeted down through the earth. Falling backwards as she landed, she banged her elbows, and pain radiated through her body. The granite ground was damp and muddy, with puddles of water scattered here and there. But the dirt ceiling had plenty of plant roots securing it, a welcome sign that it was unlikely to collapse on her.

Her heart thumping, she heard the thud of footsteps above her. Then she heard the shovel begin its work again. Steadily digging and throwing the earth away. Was Ville about to dig straight into her? Soil from the roof of the cave pattered down upon her face.

Still in shock, she was startled by a sliding sound. The sound of earth descending. Her exit route—the hole she had slipped through from the den into the cave—had begun to collapse. Tytti's heart began to thunder as the light began to fade. If she tried now, maybe she could dig herself out—right into the face of Ville Tapio. She looked over her shoulder into the cave. There was plenty of space for her to move forward, and she could see dappled light, reflections coming off the sea. She could also hear seagulls screaming. There was another way out.

Then the digging stopped. Tytti could hear nothing more. Her heart pounded. Was Ville leaving? Had he seen her? Panic surged as she crawled on her hands and knees through the mud towards the blur of light, Anna's sinister words echoing in her mind: 'No body, no crime.'

Wriggling forward, she put her head through the gap and gratefully inhaled the fresh air. She realised she could slip through the crack and climb back up the cliff.

As she turned to scramble out, her back to the opening, a shaft of deflected light shone into the long black cavern. There was something on the ground. Apprehensively, Tytti reached out and touched what seemed to be a piece of material — a thick twill cloth. Swallowing hard, she moved her hand around, feeling the pile of fabric. There was something inside it. Turning aside a fold of material, she felt skin. She snatched her hand away and gasped in horror.

Chapter Thirty-eight

Her heart racing, Tytti tentatively stepped one foot out and squeezed through the gap, using only her fingertips and toes to grasp onto the wet rock.

With the windswept clifftop above and the swell of the sea below, she had no choice but to press her body flat against the wall of slippery granite. A wave smashed against the rocks, the spray drenching her. As she tried to edge up towards the clifftop, her foot came loose, her fingertips slipped, and she lost her footing.

Choking and swallowing the briny seawater, she kicked hard and forced her head above the surface. The jagged rocks threatened, but she managed to turn and face out towards the horizon. Desperately needing to make it around the bay, she expended all her energy swimming. Would she make it? Her soaked clothes dragged her down, and her arms felt like lead. Then, thankfully, sand beneath her feet. The beach beckoned. Fighting exhaustion, she crawled forward on her hands and knees, the force of the sea trying to suck her back in. Shouting could be heard, and a crowd of people came running to pull her out.

Chapter Thirty-nine

Her rescuers had been tourists. No one needed to know what had happened yesterday.

Intent on solving the mystery, she sat back in her chair at the office and closed the email from the ballistics expert. It said that the shell was brass and came from a Luger 08, an old German weapon dating back to the 1917–1918 Finnish Civil War. Then there was a ding. Another email had come in. The forensics report from Dr Wahlroos had been sent on by Constable Mansikka-aho. Hunching forward at her screen, Tytti opened the email and started to read.

Thinking hard, she sat back in her chair. So, the bullet shell and the skull in the tree were both 100 years old. They came from the Civil War. The skull was a young man's cranium, missing a section at the back. Whoever it had belonged to was still a mystery. And the bullet shell being from the Civil War? Part of the castle had been used as a prison — this was a well-known fact. Could this bullet shell relate to the remains she had seen in the cave? Or were they indeed the remains of Heike Tapio? Anna was not going to like it, but maybe it was time to unearth the truth.

Tytti knocked on Anna's office door at the castle.

'Enter,' Anna called. Tytti tried to open the door but it would not budge. She heard a key turn and the door swung open. 'I forgot I locked it,' said Anna hurriedly. She paused and then twisted on a smile and said, 'Tytti, please sit down,' then closed the door and turned the key in the lock again. Tytti stayed standing and wondered if she should feel threatened. She had never established who had shut the flue in her cottage or run her into the ditch. But why should she be suspicious of Anna? Anna gave her another misshapen smile, and gestured for Tytti to sit. Her voice betrayed the panic she felt. 'How can I help you?'

'The threatening letters. You wrote them to yourself, didn't you? That's why you weren't worried about someone recognising your handwriting or your fingerprints matching. They'd be expected on paper you'd handled. And who would suspect you anyway? You needed a reason to call in Jari and the PI.'

'But how…?'

'At first I thought your mother, Suvi-Tuuli, had written them as her handwriting is the same as yours. Of course it would be, you're related. But then I realised that your handwriting is the same as my mother's and Ville Tapio's. Did Suvi-Tuuli home school Heike and Ville?'

'Yes… How did you…'

'My mother was also taught to write by

Suvi-Tuuli. You were all taught to write by the same person. Nurture forms the way a person writes, and in this case it did so for all three of you. Why do such a thing?'

Still standing, Anna turned her eyes to Tytti. Her hands were clenched into fists and her body rigid. Her eyes kept opening wide as she took a breath which then seemed to dissipate into her narrow frame and turn into trembling. 'I did it in a panic after Ville left. He'd just told me he was going to look for Heike's body. He read your article in the *Tapiolinna Times* and believes that the skull in the oak tree is Heike's. He thinks the police will become involved and that he will be caught.'

Tytti opened her mouth and then shut it again without saying anything. Anna did not know that the skull was not Heike's. Maybe now was not the time to tell her it was 100 years old.

'That's not true. The article about the skull didn't come out until a week later. Ville Tapio must have contacted you before the night of the hotel opening. That was when he was on the island and left the letter for me.'

'Ville was the one who asked you to look into the fire? To find the arsonist? But why?'

'I don't know. I'm yet to speak with him.'

'So, just you, me and Ville know about Heike being buried there? And nobody outside of this room knows what I've told you? Especially about the accident? Or murder. I guess it depends on how you look at things. That is correct, isn't it? Is that right? Just you and I.' She slowly edged over to the wall covered in weapons. Pausing as she got there, she reached out and ran her finger along a mace.

In a quiet voice, Tytti asked, 'How could you bury the body of the man you say you loved so cold-heartedly? I don't believe a person could do that. You weren't really in love with him, were you?'

Anna paused and looked round at Tytti. There was a distant look in her eyes. Then she sighed and said in an off-hand manner, 'I didn't love him at all.' Anna went to her desk and sat down.

'Was the baby really his?' Tytti asked watching Anna carefully.

Anna stared ahead of her, not looking at Tytti.

'No.' She paused. 'No, he wasn't the real father. The child was Karl Tapio's.'

Tytti gasped. This she had not expected. Anna jumped up again and walked across to the wall covered in guns and rifles. 'We'd had an affair when I was fifteen. I went to him when I became pregnant and he said I couldn't tell anybody that it was his. I was underage and he would have gone to prison. At the time, I considered myself a young woman able to make my own decisions. I didn't realise that he was in the wrong. Wrong to have touched me.' She took a deep breath and exhaled.

'He tossed a coin, you see, to choose which one of the twins he would have me marry. Heike never knew what his father had done. He became the cuckold. Ville never knew either. And then Terhi came along, quite luckily, ten months later.' Anna paused at a particularly robust-looking civil war handgun. 'It's the truth. I was so ashamed. I had nobody to turn to. I couldn't tell my mother. I had to go along with it.'

Tytti paused, thinking. Could Anna's mother, Suvi-Tuuli, be the reason behind Anna's behaviour? The fear of telling your mother something. The absolute shame she would have been made to feel if she had become pregnant out of wedlock? Suvi-Tuuli had indeed stated the disgust she felt about illegitimate births when fishing to find out about Tytti's own mother's situation.

'So Terhi is really Heike and Ville's half sister? If you were pregnant at fifteen then Terhi was definitely born before Karl Tapio died. That means she should have inherited half of the castle along with Ville instead of him inheriting it all.'

'Ville left the castle to me!'

'It doesn't matter and you know it. Even with a will, it would have been disregarded, and she would have inherited half. It's Finnish law. You have six months to claim your right to an inheritance. As Terhi's mother, you should have done this for her, not taken the castle from her.'

Anna hated Terhi because she was a threat to her ownership of the castle. She was, deep down, scared of her.

'And then when Ville "died" in the fire, his half should have gone to Terhi too, as she was his only living descendant. You wouldn't have been able to sell the castle and give half of the money to Ville. Even though you tricked him and kept the money for yourself.'

Anna suddenly looked very old. Her facade was crumbling. A look of shame crossed her face. A shame that she had been holding onto for many years.

She tries so hard to be perfect, thought Tytti with a sudden pang of pity. She puts all her faith in image and status. Anna was so insecure because of her past. Because of the horrible secret she had carried with her for most of her life. Tytti felt more like a counsellor than a prosecutor.

'Listen,' said Tytti, 'what you have done is wrong, very wrong. But I understand why you did it.' She may well have done the same thing. Times were different back then. Who was she to judge? 'But you have to make right this wrong. You have to give the castle to Terhi. That part of your secret must come out.'

'Well, nobody could prove it. Karl Tapio is dead,' said Anna harshly. She was not ready to relinquish her right to the castle and the profits from the hotel just yet.

'Is that really why you helped Ville? Did

you want both of the twins out of the way so you could have the castle?'

'The castle is rightfully mine!' Anna snapped. 'Having Terhi trapped me here. Why shouldn't I have it!'

'Is that why you hate Terhi so much? Stop blaming other people and take some responsibility for yourself,' Tytti chastised. She felt like she was talking to an insolent child. 'Terhi was in line to inherit the castle and her lineage can be proven. It can be established that Terhi does not have half of Heike's DNA. They can test Ville's DNA; twins have the same DNA. No, Terhi will only have one quarter of that DNA, as it comes from Karl Tapio. The other quarter would come from the Tapio twins' mother. We can't test for this, but we can discount it. Then the other half would be yours. The results of these kinds of tests are accepted by the courts.'

But then Tytti remembered: her side of the story was just a charade. And was the DNA link enough for Tytti to convince Anna to pass the castle on to Terhi? Should she tell Anna the truth? Give up the power she had over the woman? Tytti did not feel like now was the time. Maybe, instead, it was time to use that power.

'If you give Terhi back the castle, I won't write about it,' she stated.

'You won't write about it anyway,' said Anna rudely. She seemed to be back to her old self.

'You can't stop me from printing the truth if it's published in *Helsingin Sanomat.*' The scam continued.

'You wouldn't!' gasped Anna. 'I could go to prison!'

The look on Anna's face told Tytti that she had won. Should she now tell Anna the truth? That the skull was not Heike's? No. She would let her read about it in her own newspaper.

Chapter Forty

Tytti sat on the little red sofa and digested all the information at her fingertips. She had finally told Constable Mansikka-aho about the cave, and an exhumation had begun. When Anna had heard about the exhumation, she had left in a hurry for Russia, a country with no extradition agreement with Finland. Six bodies had been unearthed — that is, six sets of remains minus one head. It had not taken a great mental leap to figure out that the skull in the tree was likely to be that of the sixth man. All of them were 100 years old, which meant they dated from the Finnish Civil War, a time when Finnish prisoners of war were murdered by men who may well have been their next-door neighbours.

Dr Wahlroos added that she had conducted a further check against DNA taken from possible relatives to find the men's families. This had, so far, identified five of the six men, whose families confirmed that they had fought for the Reds during the Civil War. They had all been Finns, not Russians. All had been agrarian workers fighting for their livelihood.

Tytti sipped her coffee and pondered her earlier conversation with Constable Mansikka-aho and Dr Wahlroos over at the police station.

'They were all young men. Teenagers, really. A sad situation, for them to be treated so roughly,' said Dr Wahlroos, showing unexpected emotion. Then she continued in a far more professional tone. 'The remains cannot tell us whether a person was fat or thin, but the fact that the circumference of the belts was so small indicates that they would have been extremely malnourished. They may also have been diseased, suffering from Spanish Flu: at the time, the prisons were rife with it. From the rope, we can tell that their wrists had been tied behind them before they were shot in the back of the head. A *coup de grâce*. We found the rope, as the area is peat and peat will preserve such things as clothes and rope for a long time. The peat also explains the preservation of skin, hair and internal organs. A body submerged in a peat bog will not rot. The peat is acidic and contains little oxygen, so the microorganisms that cause decay cannot survive. It seems that the White forces executed the Red prisoners and then marked them down as missing or fallen in battle. Sadly, the people in this grave seem to have been such victims. As for how they got into the cave, I have no idea.'

'It's possible,' said Tytti, 'the area was boggy until quite recently, before the copse really took over. It would definitely have been a bog 100 years ago. It would not yet have been frozen like the ground, since ground freezes before bog. It would have been the easiest place to dispose of the bodies if the assassinations took place during the winter — and the Civil War did take place in the winter. The cave I fell into was wet with seawater. As saltwater and peat don't mix, like an acid and a base, the seawater from the recent summer storms must have got into the copse and caused it to collapse into the cave. It would explain the dampness, and the hollow in the copse.'

'Entirely possible,' said Constable Mansikka-aho. 'In fact, now you mention it, that seems like the most likely scenario.' He was relieved that he would not have to investigate further. 'But the skull. How did it get into the tree? Who put it there?'

'It's possible,' speculated Tytti. 'The skull could have fallen into the sea from the opening of the cave — you did say it had become demineralised by seawater,' Tytti said to Dr Wahlroos. 'From there, it could easily have been picked up by a bird which then dropped it in the tree. The small puncture marks under the eye sockets of the skull — those could have been made by the claws of a bird. I don't think anybody put it in the tree at all. My instinct is that it's a coincidence.'

Chapter Forty-one

Risto stood behind the lectern and quietly arranged the pages of his sermon. For the occasion, he had chosen to wear a white chasuble and light blue stole, a flattering combination that was further set off by the surroundings, an altarpiece painted teal and gold, dawn-till-dusk blues surrounding golden angels under the overhead arches, and an oil painting of Jesus and his disciples behind the altar. A grand representation of God's glory.

The church was built in the 14th century. The walls were painted grey stone. Waves of oak pews bathed in yellow light stood upon the flagstones. Brass knobs, like prostrate pawns, protruded from the backs of pews for bags to hang on. Faded red velvet kneeling-stools stood by patiently on the flagstones. The smell was of bitter old wood.

The elaborately carved tombs of the wealthy dead sat cheek by jowl with the struggling living. While the dead outnumbered the living, the usual feeling of quiet calm felt gloomy, and the high vaulted ceiling threatened to crash down upon you rather than elevate you to heaven.

There were hushed whispers, then silence.

The rustle of a plastic bag, a cough, a sniff. Then, echoing footsteps, and the wail of wood as a door to a pew was opened and a new member arrived. As more people ambled in, the gloom lifted and the austere space began to feel small and cosy. A church without people is just an empty mausoleum.

Tytti sat with cold hands, and surveyed the pews. The church was far from full. Surely a commemoration for the war dead was an important affair to attend? But then, in today's climate, maybe soldiers and war were not to be glorified. By many, war was now viewed to be the failure of mankind. The Lutherans who did make it to church, usually came for a christening, confirmation, wedding or funeral.

Why not have divorces held in churches too? wondered Tytti. All the angry parties (mothers-in-law; mistresses) sitting together in church. The vicar allocating the children here, the dog there... Tytti smiled to herself.

Then there was the issue of Finland being one of the most heavily armed countries on the planet. The third — at least, when she had last checked the statistics.

All of us peace-loving Lutherans carrying guns — it doesn't quite make sense, thought Tytti. Then again, most shoot-outs seemed to happen when a man decided to murder his family and then turn the gun on himself. As if he believed in heaven and expected them all to relocate there. Or, and probably more likely, he couldn't bear to share them. Had to take them with him so they could never move on and have happy lives. She did not believe that these men hated their family. Their wife, their children...

Ritva slid along the pew next to her and disturbed Tytti's maudlin thoughts. Lili barked, as an old lady in a black beret walked past, and then lay down nicely next to Ritva.

One man sat alone, his dark hair wet-combed over to one side. He wore thick round glasses and his bible was open on the pew in front of him. He glanced at it, then looked around. The lady with the black beret sat down near him and opened her bible too.

Then Risto began.

There were many unknown people in the congregation. Finnish families, come by reason of shared DNA to mourn the loss of a relative, one of the exhumed soldiers, ready to be taken home.

'It's curious,' whispered Ritva into Tytti's ear, 'we wouldn't be free if it wasn't for the Reds fighting. And your dad would never have been able to be a vicar, him not being noble and a White.'

'Yes,' whispered Tytti back. 'And a good thing they managed to abolish the large estates and create peasant freeholds. Imagine the mess we'd be in if we still lived in a feudal society. No democracy!'

After the service Risto stood by the door, said a few words and shook people's hands as they departed. As she left, Tytti walked across to look at the war memorial and the blue- and white-ribboned wreath that had been placed beneath it. The unknown soldier was going to be interred in a military graveyard in Lappeenranta on the mainland.

War. Humanity's failure, she thought. Sometimes she got caught up in believing in war out of respect for her own family's war dead. But every time it failed. Had there ever been a successful war? The victims would be the first to say from their graves:

Don't fight, it wasn't worth it, I missed out on my life, murdered by a stranger.

Chapter Forty-two

Tytti decided to walk over to the vicarage to wait for her father. Up in her old bedroom, she sat on the bed and picked up her old teddy bear, Winston.

'Hello, Winnie,' she said. 'What has been going on up here then?' Half of her bedroom had, in her absence, become an office space, stacked to the rafters with boxes of files. Her father's computer sat on a desk next to the window. Could she really invade her father's privacy in order to find out the truth?

So it seemed.

Tytti went over and sat at the computer. Typing in the password, she apologised to God and began to scroll. There it was, Ville Tapio's name. She noticed that the time and date were the same as those written on Ville's notepad, the notepad she had seen in his boat. Engrossed in her findings, Tytti did not see her father returning up the path through the window.

According to his diary, her father had been helping Ville rather than Anna. He did have feelings for Anna, but they were, at that time, probably not friendly ones. Tytti was just about to read on.

'I see you're as inquisitive as ever.'

Tytti jumped at her father's voice, and turned from the screen.

'Dad, have you ever spoken to a man called Ville Tapio?'

Risto stiffened and looked shiftily at the ground.

Is he about to lie? thought Tytti, shocked. Then he looked up.

'I don't know how much you've read, but if I tell you this you *must* keep it confidential. I'm only going to tell you if you promise to do that.'

Pausing for a second to think about the article she wanted to write, Tytti quickly conceded before her father had time to reflect.

'I promise,' she said. And a promise to her father meant something.

'A man phoned one evening. It was quite late. He wouldn't tell me his name but he asked to come and see me so we made an appointment for the next day. When he arrived, the first thing he told me was that he was Ville Tapio. I could barely believe it. I thought the man an imposter, but as he talked on he described his previous life at the castle and I began to believe him. It was quite a shock. He went on to tell me the story of Heike's death. A tragic accident, so it seemed. Do I have to repeat this to you?'

Tytti shook her head.

'He told me that he ran wild as a teenager. He drank, he gambled—disappeared for days, frittering away his money. He said he had run up debts with some very dangerous people, so he and Anna hatched an outlandish scheme. A scheme that only scared teenagers would come up with. They planned the fire at the castle and to fake Ville's death. He willed the castle to Anna so that the insurance money would go to her, and then she would give half to him. But Anna double-crossed him. She told him that the castle was now hers and there was nothing he could do about it. She kept the insurance money and restored the castle. He was stuck — in no position to argue, as he was officially dead. He had to quietly leave the island, without a penny to his name.'

Awed by these revelations, Tytti sat on the edge of her seat and began to realise just how much Anna had lied to her — unless Ville was lying. But then, her father was a good judge of character.

'As you can imagine, he was in quite a state. He'd wanted to come forward about the accident for years and when the castle had its opening event, well, he thought it was an opportunity for him to return to the island unseen. He went to Anna and told her that he wanted to confess. She said no, that nobody would believe him, as there was no body. She said that nobody would believe an arsonist who had faked his own death over her.'

'And that was when he left a letter for me. He wanted me to investigate, prove his story and expose Anna.'

'That's right. He told me about recruiting

you. But when he read your report about the skull in the tree he panicked. He immediately thought it was Heike's, and a sign from God. For years he had been feeling guilt over Heike's death. He thought it was his fault. That if they hadn't argued, Heike would still be alive today. So he started to search for the body.'

'He never demanded a penny from Anna, did he? And that's why he's been looking for Heike's body. He doesn't want to destroy it at all.'

'Destroy it? No, he wants to uncover it and give it a proper burial. He is ready to repent. I told him that he didn't need to expose himself and Anna in order to do that; that this was a conversation to be held between him and God. Only God could — and would — forgive him. I convinced him to leave the island and continue with the new life he had made for himself in Estonia rather than go to prison, possibly taking Anna along with him.'

Tytti paused to think. Ville Tapio was not a monster after all. He had become a man of God.

Chapter Forty-three

The next morning, Tytti returned to the office and was hanging up her cardigan when the door was wrenched open. Suvi-Tuuli stood there. Her head was tilted back and her jaw thrust forward. Her eyes were angry and clouded.

'You had to delve, didn't you? You had to dig up the truth!'

'It was you, wasn't it?' said Tytti calmly. 'It was you that told the police about my father and Miina.'

'Yes, I saw them together at church. I could just tell by the look of her. I knew there was something going on. People don't notice me, but I notice everything. How disgusting for a vicar to be with a harlot. Prostitution is a sin!' spat Suvi-Tuuli. 'And *you*. Accusing me of being involved in a crime. How dare you! I would never commit a crime, I'm a Christian!'

Tytti thought back regretfully to the day she had accused Suvi-Tuuli; she had let the dislike she felt for the old woman cloud her judgement. Deep down she had known that Suvi-Tuuli was not the culprit. She had just wanted revenge on her for the things she had said about her father. She had wanted to make her the perpetrator.

'Anna has told me everything about her

past. She had to, in order to explain how she lost the castle. I have disowned her. Disgusting girl. How could she be unmarried and be with Karl Tapio? And then the affair with Ulrich Tolliver going on all these years. She was probably unmarried when she was first with Heike and Simo, too! All the opportunities she has had, and look what she's done with them. Wasted every one of them. She and her stupid family. Terhi is just like her mother, Kai is an idiot, and who knows how the younger ones will develop. What a waste! If I'd had the opportunities they had, I would have made something of myself! Instead I had to be a teacher. And now I have to paint to become well known!' Her head tossed back, Suvi-Tuuli laughed nastily.

What a woman, thought Tytti. Suddenly, a memory flashed into her mind. Kai and Terhi had been devastated when the puppy they had been given for Christmas died of poisoning before the New Year. Suvi-Tuuli had been quite vocal about her dislike for dogs. Dirty creatures, she had called them. Once, when they had been playing, the puppy had run up to Suvi-Tuuli and she, thinking nobody was watching her, had hit it. Could Suvi-Tuuli have been the poisoner? She was certainly capable of it, thought Tytti. All these years I've thought her to be kind. I admired her and trusted her. And it was all a sham. A disguise for a black heart.

Tytti had underestimated the depth of Suvi-Tuuli's act. But this was the true Suvi-Tuuli now. A woman full of hatred and bitterness.

'And *you*! Always hanging around my family. With your whiter-than-white reputation. No one can be that good. I don't know your secrets, but I will uncover them one day!'

Tytti thought back to the conversation they had had about her father. Oh no, she won't, thought Tytti. There is nothing to uncover.

'Is this what being a Lutheran means to you?' said Tytti quietly. 'To reject your own daughter because she had sex before marriage? You are blindly following the bible without applying an ounce of common sense. Just because you don't like sex doesn't mean you should make it biblical to justify yourself. You're just another Lutheran who has been sexually repressed by a religious education! Forget the fact that many of the men in the Old Testament were polygamous. The Bible advocated monogamy only for religious leaders. Otherwise, the men had a choice back then. It didn't matter how many wives or concubines they had. Only if they had sex with a married woman was it considered sinful. However, only the woman could be stoned to death for it. If women had equally been allowed to be polygamous, there would not even have been a problem. And frankly, all those times Anna was unmarried or divorced she wouldn't even have been committing a sin if one was to apply the same biblical principle that only a married woman can sin...'

Tytti's mind wandered, and she remembered once reading in her father's notes about a young couple who had just moved to the island. They had visited her father to ask if they could still take communion even though they already lived together but were not to be married for another month. Her father had noted his thoughts.

'The Lutheran Church says that a requirement for the proper reception of Communion is that a person is not guilty of wilful sin. Is being in love and living together a wilful sin? Or is that love a gift from God?'

He had not mentioned how he had solved his dilemma.

'How dare you!' shouted Suvi-Tuuli in shock. Nobody had ever challenged her religious beliefs like that. She was spitting fire, and her religious fervour was turning towards violence. 'You watch your back, young lady. I'll get something on you yet!' Clenching her jaw and fists, she stormed out of the office, her threat hanging in mid-air.

Chapter Forty-four

Tytti and Ritva sat together on the bench outside the coffee shop. This lull in the day was a good time to swap viewpoints on life. Lili, who needed a trim, was vigorously scratching her ear.

After pleasantries had been exchanged, Ritva went on: 'So, the coffee shop is not going to be shut down. There was a mass protest outside the Parliament House, and the law has been changed, so that dogs can be inside cafés so long as they don't go in the kitchen,' she said happily. Lili was free to wander.

'That's excellent news!' Ritva's passivity in dealing with the situation had paid off.

After swatting away a bothersome seagull, Tytti steered the conversation her way.

'Teemu has gone quiet. I think that means he's too drunk to bother to communicate,' she said harshly, before correcting herself. 'I don't really mean that, I just think the stress of his wife leaving him, along with the paper maybe closing down, has fried his nerves. I'm worried too.' Then she decided it was time to raise a sensitive topic again. 'How... er... has it been going with Kai?' Tytti asked the question carefully. Ritva had been silent on the subject for a while. Now she stared at the tablecloth.

'The accident. After the helicopter crash, I began to realise something. I realised that I liked Kai. I was far more distraught than a person should have been — that's if I'd been the kind of person who only wanted to marry for money.' Ritva half looked up at Tytti to gauge her response.

Thank goodness, thought Tytti, she has finally realised she was wrong to behave as she did.

'I see him as a friend now. I'm going to break up with him. I'm just going to wait until he's feeling better.'

Across the market square, Teemu and his wife sat in high-backed, overstuffed chairs at a little table in the window of Strindberg's. Streams of sunlight illuminated the cobblestones outside, but the couple was protected from the glare by a black canopy. Earlier that day, a group of irate yoginis had cornered the yoga guru and prised it out of him that he was having affairs with several of them. He had told each of them to keep it a secret, but had been caught out when two of the women had gossiped. When the yelling had subsided, he had slunk off to pack up his equipment. Dealing with the women had been bad enough; he was not about to hang around for the furious husbands. And now two of the aforesaid sat opposite each other: an estranged husband and wife. Neither was able to make eye contact for long, instead looking out at the market square. The guilty wife began the conversation. She asked Teemu to take her back. He looked at her in astonishment. And then the tears came. He said yes, and his wife placed her hand over his.

Chapter Forty-five

Tytti had called the forensic archaeologist and disliked his conduct on the phone. He had impressed on her how busy he was and that he would be doing her an immense favour by letting her come to see him.

But he might be less difficult in person, she thought. He might simply have no phone manners. Perhaps an unfortunate upbringing. He might be one of those.

The bus dropped her off at a stop in front of Helsinki's main department store, Stockmann. As it was a nice day, she decided to take a small detour and walk around the corner and down through the esplanade. Looking out for trams, she crossed the road and, stopping at an ice-cream stand, picked up a vanilla-flavoured Eskimo ice cream, her favourite since childhood.

Once in the flower-filled park that had been laid out by Engel, Tytti walked over to her favourite statue, *Fact and Fable*, a memorial to the children's writer Zacharias Topelius. The two bronze women stood opposite each other. One woman, named Fact, held a vertical lick of flame, the flame of truth, in the palm of her hand. The other, Fable, held the cartoon-like bird of fables, with its crowned head, on her fingertip. Among other things, Topelius had been a journalist, a proper journalist, and Tytti admired him.

Turning to her left, she began to walk down the Esplanade Park. Hundreds of people were lazing about on the parched grass, holidaymakers and lunching office workers. Others swathed the benches, all of them drenched in sunshine, babies laughing, children playing, trying to catch iridescent bubbles made by a street performer. Tytti reached the centre of the park and paused to look at the naturalistic statue of Runeburg. There he stood, frozen in time, unable to begin his song — the national anthem of Finland. Tytti read the verses of the anthem inscribed on the statue. Beginning to whistle the chorus, she continued her walk until the music from a jazz band playing on the outdoor stage overtook her. Tossing her ice-cream stick into a bin, she came to the fountain near the market square, and to the flirty nude statue of Havis Amanda. Tytti paused to take a look.

Why are so many artists perverts? she asked herself. With an aversion to female clothing. Designed by men, for men. No, that's unfair, thought Tytti, correcting herself. There are a few statues of male nudes in Helsinki. Probably by men, for men, she added, thinking of the gay icon, *Tom of Finland*. Well, she was no artist and no critic.

Turning to the left and crossing a cobbled street, she walked up a narrow lane, past pastel-painted buildings of pink, yellow and blue, towards Senate Square. The square was dominated by an overbearing white Lutheran cathedral with the twelve apostles dotted around the ledge of the roof, watching over the city. She walked across the old graveyard, now a cobbled square in front of the cathedral, the graves only metres below. Pausing for a moment, she looked at the statue of the friendly Russian Emperor, Alexander II, still allowed to occupy his plinth almost 100 years after Finland gained independence from a fallen Russian Empire. Government Palace was to her right and the University building to her left. This was the original university and the habitat of one forensic archaeologist, Dr Anseli Aho, PhD.

Tytti asked the porter the whereabouts of his office and found it to be on the top floor. Being an old building, it had elegant marble stairs, and sculptures at every turn of the landing. But no lift. By the time Tytti got to the top she was puffed out. Not noticing the anatomically correct male genitals of a Roman emperor right next to her face, she leaned on a pedestal and paused to take a break. Reaching the top, Tytti knocked on the door.

Side-parted, gelled hair. Pointed shoes that tapped. A bounce in his step. These were Tytti's first impressions of Dr Anseli Aho. After a brief introduction, Aho stated, 'I don't have much time so let's get on with it.'

'Bullet. Denis found a bullet that led to a

Civil War grave being discovered. He deserves a place on your course.'

'And why is this not on his application?'

'At the time, we didn't know where the bullet came from. It was only after Professor —, a ballistics expert (I'm sure you know of him), analysed it for us that we could be sure.' Tytti had decided to name-drop, and for the first time Aho looked up at her with a modicum of interest.

'And what is your connection with the application?'

'I am the referee.'

Aho flicked the cover page over and began to read what Tytti had written.

'This application was delivered late.'

'Yes, and it explains on the application why that is the case.' An explanation about the long wait for social services had been added.

'The boy seems somewhat weak-minded.' Tytti flushed with embarrassment.

'Well, he isn't,' she snapped, finally having had enough of Aho's attitude.

Aho looked up at her with condescension in his eyes. This woman obviously had no self-control. Hormones probably. Well, he did prefer to have men on the course, for this very reason. Although the presence of a pretty girl now and again, to spice things up a bit, did not hurt.

'Leave it with me,' he said suddenly, and rose to open the door. As it slammed shut behind Tytti, she stood in the hallway beside a glass case full of skulls. They had been stashed here together with no consideration for burial rites—just an ugly display of human remains.

What a way to end up, thought Tytti, one's skull on display in a glass box.

Chapter Forty-six

The benefit at the church had been organised to raise money for a new children's hospital. At the last minute, Terhi had offered the use of the castle, free of charge, since it was larger and thus able to accommodate more guests and, ultimately, raise more money. She was beginning to enjoy her new-found authority.

Terhi was feeling much better. She had just spent an awkward afternoon with her mother, Anna. Anna had explained to her the unpleasant history of the castle's ownership and how and why Terhi had been duped as a child. Then they had met with a solicitor to have the castle signed over to her. Terhi was about to ask how Anna could have lied to her for all these years when she suddenly thought better of it and decided not to question her mother's motives. Her mother had never appreciated that. She could be unpredictable, and this moment of generosity could be immediately rescinded. And her mother was being nice to her, and this meant a lot to Terhi. In truth, it was because Anna felt vulnerable and wanted to keep on living at the castle, but Terhi had no intention of throwing her out. She loved her mother.

It seems that the right attitude *is* everything, thought Terhi. Tytti had been right. We all get dragged through our parents' lives. But we cannot simply inherit their problems. A line has to be drawn, occasionally a wall built, with the past placed firmly behind it.

She had also agreed to bail out the newspaper.

A hyperactive Master of Ceremonies began the programme by introducing a well-known baritone, a bald man with spectacles whose appearance belied his exquisite singing voice. Then a group of violinists from a local school came on stage.

'They are to play the violin by ear only!' exclaimed the MC. This worked well enough until a few of the children forgot the music and had no sheet to refer to.

Maybe they could have been given a choice — allowed to use sheet music if they wanted it, thought Tytti. Or is giving children a choice too progressive for schools? Even Finnish schools?

For the finale, the local school children sang a few Eurovision numbers, including Israel's winning entry of 1979, 'Hallelujah', a well-known song that the audience sang along to.

'Yes, the seats are wonderfully comfortable,' agreed Tytti, gazing around the hall as she chatted to Teemu's wife, adding, 'And I'm very happy for you both.' She had just been told that

Teemu and his wife were moving back to Kuopio, where they were from, in the hope of rekindling their marriage. As they walked into a separate room where coffee and cake was being handed out, a thought suddenly struck Tytti. If Teemu quits the newspaper, who will replace him? The role called for more journalistic experience than Kai. Maybe a new editor was imminent, then. Tytti groaned inside.

'I suppose you could take over?' said Teemu in an off-hand manner.

For the first time in a long time, Tytti was speechless. After agreeing to negotiate her new salary at a later date, she noticed Ritva talking to a man. A man who looked rather like the man from the council.

'Excuse me a moment,' said Tytti, wanting in on this conversation.

Ritva's head was inclined towards the man's as she listened politely.

'Yes, the *haliaeetus albicilla* or Finnish White Eagle primarily builds its nests on rocky ledges on sea cliffs or in high trees. In a fork between branches, usually, or near the trunk. Each pair has two or three nests, so my next step is to begin searching for the others. This one pair seems to have settled in. They take their prey from the surface of quiet waters, so the bay area is perfect for them...' The man from the council rambled on.

On the bicycle ride home, Tytti suddenly felt it

was time, and sharply turned her handlebars to take the lane towards the church. Leaning her battered bicycle against a mossy stone wall, she walked between the old headstones to a newer one in the corner. It was Henri's grave.

I loved you all along, she thought; but since your death, because of that woman, I have told myself that I hated you. So much so that I did start to hate you. I can't bear to feel that way about you anymore, so, I'm forgiving you.

And she turned and walked away.

Back at home, she looked around a chilly and unwelcoming room and decided to sit out on the porch for a while. It was a humid night, and sleep would be difficult. Twisting the cold metal handle of the warped and rickety door, Tytti went out onto the porch and sat down on the battered swing seat, carelessly jerking the chain with her bodyweight. Dropping a sandal from each foot, she stared out at the translucent pink glow of the horizon. A soft pink smudge, luminous white at the brightest point, dividing an unruffled indigo sky.

The rusty chains squeaked as Tytti swung back and forth, her thoughts emptying away. As the sun came out from behind a puff of cloud, the ocean twinkled up at her. She smiled, got up and went inside to put some music on. A seagull sang along to Mozart's *Die Maurerfreude*.

Chapter Forty-seven

Tytti sat on the little red sofa with a new mug of coffee. It was a vibrantly colourful mug, splashed with large pink and red poppies — a mug she felt suited her new status as Editor.

Life was good. Kai and Ulrich had talked. Ulrich had told Kai that he was, in fact, his father. Kai had been shocked, and then elated, as he had never really liked Simo. Tytti was glad that she had not had to be the bearer of this news. From now on she would stay out of anything personal to do with Kai.

And then there was Anna Tapio. A woman of forty-five who had had four different children by three different men. Well, that was as far as Tytti knew. She paused and wondered for a moment about JoJo's dark hair and green eyes, and then decided to mind her own business. Surely, having children by several men should no longer be an issue. Neither men nor women were primarily known for their monogamous instincts, and a woman could always pick up another man for the job. Tytti thought back to that Swedish TV presenter who had four different kids by four different men. She was quite open about the fact, and indeed proud of it. But Anna. A woman who seemingly had it all had been at the centre of decades of lies and deceit. Anna valued trust above all, though not truthfulness. Lies were second nature to her. Or at least they had been. Tytti wondered if she had learned anything at all from her recent experiences. For her own part, Tytti had yet to see any change.

Who had shot the men was still unknown and unlikely to be discovered. Who would come forward to admit to such a crime? Or the culprit could be long dead. That pit of dead bodies had been well hidden: dug never to be discovered.

After all that digging with Denis, no silver had been found. Not to mention Heike Tapio's body. Ville had left due to Risto's counsel. The skull in the tree had not been a message from God to him. If it had been, things might have turned out very differently for Anna.

Her father had been right. There were grey areas. Places where a white lie here and there could be an asset. Yes, things had gone grey for a while; the border between right and wrong, between black and white, had become blurred. And she had found herself surrounded by ethical dilemmas — unsure of what was the right thing to do. But then the solutions had come quite naturally. She had simply to listen to her conscience. Wait for that quiet voice to speak. The quiet voice she had shut out for so long by being so cynical.

She thought of her deceased boyfriend. Then she checked her emotions. No: there was no misery there. Forgiving her boyfriend had brought her not happiness but emptiness. Now she understood that the bitterness she had felt towards him had been seeping into her everyday life. Into other relationships, with her family and friends. How paranoid she had been — to believe that people were trying to asphyxiate her or run her over!

She smiled to herself. Really, it was all about just working out a way to be.

Well, she thought, off to Strindberg, then. Teemu was having a leaving do there, and Tytti was looking forward to saying goodbye to him. She felt a moment of guilt for feeling that way, but it quickly passed. Then she jumped at a bang on the window.

'I got in!' Denis was outside waving a letter in his hand. It seemed that Aho had been rude but fair, after all. Denis mimed something about heading to Strindberg and then whizzed off on his moped, brimming with joy.

So Finland was Finland, with its rules and regulations and inordinate number of road signs... but people were still people in all their glory, greed and self-serving ways. Those rules and regulations did not stop them. Temptation was rife, in this case: gambling, sex and thievery. Tytti had habitually thought it best to let temptation run its course: wait for the feeling to disappear without acting upon it. That was what her father had taught her anyway. A worthy lesson to have learned. One only had to look at what happened when such wisdom was ignored.

Epilogue

It was the first day of the new administration. Tytti arrived at work with a smile on her face. Fortunately, she had managed to catch up with the young woman who had inquired about an internship; thus, the position was already filled, and the gurgle of the coffee machine awaited her.

The intern sat at her new desk. She had been shocked and then amused when the job offer came in. She had spent so much time and effort trying to make this happen, and then it had just fallen into her lap. She had written the letter of complaint for the Editor to read, but it had either failed to reach him or had been ignored. Then she had upped her game and tried to asphyxiate that Tytti Vertainen so she could get her Staff Writer's job. When that had also failed, she had tried to run her over. Yes, from the day she went into the newspaper office to leave her CV—chiefly to take a good look at Tytti—she had been trying to create opportunities that would bring her the job she desired. She was determined to become a journalist, even though she lacked the privileges of Tytti Vertainen. Look at her—hanging around with those rich Tapios. No, she would not allow anyone to stand in her way; she was determined to make her own luck.